Anonymous

Revised Charter and Ordinances of the City of Ann Arbor

SALZWASSER
VERLAG

Anonymous

Revised Charter and Ordinances of the City of Ann Arbor

Reprint of the original, first published in 1859.

1st Edition 2022 | ISBN: 978-3-37512-140-2

Verlag (Publisher): Salzwasser Verlag GmbH, Zeilweg 44, 60439 Frankfurt, Deutschland
Vertretungsberechtigt (Authorized to represent): E. Roepke, Zeilweg 44, 60439 Frankfurt, Deutschland
Druck (Print): Books on Demand GmbH, In de Tarpen 42, 22848 Norderstedt, Deutschland

REVISED CHARTER

AND

ORDINANCES

OF THE

CITY OF ANN ARBOR.

PUBLISHED BY ORDER OF THE COMMON COUNCIL.

ANN ARBOR:

E. B. POND, CITY PRINTER.

1859.

INDEX TO THE CHARTER.

Officers of the City Ann Arbor
FOR 1859—60.

———

MAYOR,...ROBERT J. BARRY.

RECORDER,...NORVAL E. WELCH.

*ALDERMEN—FIRST WARD,......ANDREW J. SUTHERLAND, WILLIAM McCREERY.

" SECOND WARD,................JACOB WIEL, HERMANN SCHLACK.

" THIRD WARD,....................DANIEL HISCOCK, THOMAS EARL.

'. FOURTH WARD,...............RICHARD HOOPER, ELIHU B. POND.

MARSHAL,..STEPHEN WEBSTER.

TREASURER,..LEWIS C. RISDON.

STREET COMMISSIONER,....................................JOSEPH BEST.

CITY ATTORNEY,..HIRAM J. BEAKES.

SUPERVISOR—FIRST AND SECOND WARDS,......................CONRAD KRAPF.

" THIRD AND FOURTH " ....JAMES H. MORRIS.

JUSTICE OF THE PEACE,...........EARL P. GARDINER. Term expires July 4, 1860.

" " ....GILBERT SHATTUCK. Term expires July 4, 1861.

" " .....CHURCHILL H. VANCLEVE. Term expires July 4, 1862.

" " ....WILLIAM F. ROTH. Term expires July 4, 1863.

CONSTABLE—FIRST WARD,..............................WILLIAM A. HATCH.

" SECOND WARD,.................................EMIL OSIANDER.

" THIRD WARD,..............................THOMAS J. HOSKINS.

" FOURTH WARD,................................HENRY BINDER.

SCHOOL INSPECTOR,.............WARREN J JACKSON. Term expires April, 1860.

" " ....DANIEL S. TWITCHELL. Term expires April, 1861.

———

MAYORS OF ANN ARBOR SINCE ITS INCORPORATION.

April, 1851 to April, 1838.............................GEORGE SEDGWICK.

" 1853 " " 1855.............................EDWIN R. TREMAIN.

'. 1855 " " 1856.............................JAMES KINGSLEY.

" 1856 " " 1858.............................WILLIAM S. MAYNARD.

" 1858 " " 1859.............................PHILIP BACH.

" 1859 " ....ROBERT J. BARRY.

*The term of office of the Alderman first named in each ward, expires in 1860, and of the second, in 1861.

CHARTER.

NOTE.—Sections 4, 5, 6, 7, 9, 11, 12, 16, 17, 20, 24, 25, 33, 39, and 40, embrace the amendments made by the Act of 1859, and are inserted in place of the corresponding sections of the original Act of 1851, of which they are amendatory.

An ACT to incorporate the City of Ann Arbor.

SECTION 1. *The People of the State of Michigan enact,* That so much of the Township of Ann Arbor, in the County of Washtenaw, as is included in the following limits, to wit : All of section twenty-nine, and all those portions of the south half of section twenty, the south-west quarter of section twenty-one, and the west half of section twenty-eight which lie southerly and westerly of the north bank of the Huron River, be and the same is hereby set off from said township, and declared to be a City, by the name of the " City of Ann Arbor."

SEC. 2. The freemen of said City, from time to time being inhabitants thereof, shall be and continue to be, a body corporate and politic, by the name of the " Mayor, Recorder and Aldermen of the City of Ann Arbor ;" and by that name they shall be known in law, and shall be capable of suing and being sued, and of prosecuting and defending all suits ; they may have a common seal, which they may alter at pleasure, and shall be capable of purchasing, holding, conveying and disposing of real and personal estate for the use of said corporation.

SEC. 3. The said City shall be divided into four wards, as follows : The First Ward shall embrace all that portion of the City lying east of Main street and south of Huron street : the Second Ward shall embrace all that portion of the City lying south of Huron street and west of Main street ; the Third Ward shall embrace all that portion of the City lying north of Huron street and west of Fourth street ; and the Fourth Ward shall embrace all that portion of the City lying north of Huron street and east of Fourth street. The aforesaid division is made by the actual or supposed continuation of the center line of each of said streets, in the present direction thereof, to the limits of the City : *Provided*, That the Common Council may at any time alter the bounds of either of said wards.

SEC. 4. There shall be the following officers in and for said City, to wit : One Mayor ; one Recorder ; one Marshal ; one Street Commissioner ; one Attorney ; two Supervisors—one in the First and Second wards, and one in the Third and Fourth wards—who shall be Assessors in their respective districts ; one Treasurer, who shall also be Collector ; and four Constables, one to be elected in each ward—who [all of which officers] shall hold their offices for one year, and until their successors are elected and qualified ; eight Aldermen, two to be elected in each ward ; two School Inspectors, and two Directors of the Poor, who shall respectively hold their offices for one and two years, and until their successors are elected and qualified ; and four Justices of the Peace, who shall respectively hold their offices for four years.

SEC. 5. The inhabitants of said City having the qualifications of electors under the constitution of this State, shall, on the first Monday of April, at such place in each ward as the Common Council shall designate, proceed to elect, by a plurality of votes, by ballot, from among the qualified electors of said City, one Mayor, one Recorder, one Justice of the Peace, one Marshal, one Street Commissioner, one Treasurer and Collector, one School Inspector, and one Director of the Poor ; and the inhabitants of each ward in said City having the like qualifications of electors, shall, at such place in each ward as the Common Council shall designate, at the same time proceed to elect an Alderman and one Constable ; and there shall also at the same time be elected, one Supervisor by the qualified electors of the First and Second wards, and one Supervisor by the qualified electors of the Third and Fourth wards : *Provided*, That at the election to be holden on the first Monday of April, eighteen hundred and fifty-nine, there shall be elected two Aldermen in each ward in which there shall be no Alderman already elected and having another year to serve, and one Alderman in each of the other wards ; *and Provided also*, That such Justice, Supervisor, Constables, Treasurer, School Inspectors, and Directors of the Poor, shall each of them have the like power, and be subject to the same duties and liabilities as such officers respectively in the several townships of this State ; *and Provided further*, that all actions within the jurisdiction of Justices of the Peace may be commenced and prosecuted in said Justices' Courts, when the plaintiff or defendant, or one of the plaintiffs or defendants resides in a township next adjoining the township of Ann Arbor, or the township of York, Saline, Freedom or Lima.

Sec. 6. Immediately after the election to be held on the first Monday of April, eighteen hundred and fifty-nine, the Aldermen of those wards in which two shall have been elected as hereinbefore provided, shall divide themselves into classes, so that the term of office of one Alderman in each ward composing the first class shall expire at the end of one year, and of the other Alderman in each ward composing the second class, at the end of two years, and one Alderman shall thereafter be elected annually in each ward to hold his office for two years, and until his successor is elected and qualified. Each Alderman shall reside in the ward for which he is elected, and on the removal of any Alderman from such ward he shall vacate his office.

Sec. 7. At the first election to be holden under this act as amended hereby, there shall be chosen *viva voce*, by the electors present, two judges and a clerk of the election, at the place designated for the holding of such election in each ward, and such judges and clerk shall, before proceeding to the discharge of their duties, make and [subscribe] an oath or affirmation faithfully and impartially to discharge the duties of their respective offices at such election—which oath or affirmation may be administered by any person authorized to administer oaths ; and at all subsequent elections the two Aldermen in each ward shall be the judges in case they shall attend, and a clerk shall be appointed by the Aldermen or judges of election at all elections in each ward. In case such Aldermen or either of them fail to attend or to act as judges, judges of election shall be chosen by the electors present in the manner above provided for the first election, and shall be qualified in like manner. At the close of the polls, the votes shall be canvassed, and a statement thereof proclaimed by one of the judges, and a correct record of the number of votes given for each person shall be made by the clerk and signed officially by the persons holding the election, and filed with the Recorder. It shall be the duty of the Common Council to meet, as soon as conveniently may be, after such election, to canvass the votes cast in the respective wards, and to declare and certify the result of such canvass.

Sec. 8. It shall be the duty of the Recorder, or in case of his neglect so to do, then of the Mayor, to cause five days' notice of every election to be given, by posting up written or printed notices thereof in five or more public places in said City : *Provided*, That if notice of any election shall not be given as herein required, it shall be lawful for the electors to meet at the proper time and place and hold the election ; and in case of the non-attendance or neglect of the proper officers to act, the electors present may *viva voce* choose persons to act in their places ; *and Provided also*, That if any election of officers under this act shall not be made on the day when it ought to have been made, the said corporation shall not for that cause be dissolved ; but it shall be lawful to hold such election at any time thereafter, public notice thereof being given as provided in this act. At all elections the polls shall be opened between the hours of nine and eleven o'clock in the forenoon, and be closed at four o'clock in the afternoon.

Sec. 9. Every person offering to vote at any election in said City shall, if required by any elector present, before he shall be permitted to vote, take the following oath or affirmation before one of the judges of such election : " I do solemnly swear (or affirm) that I am a citizen of the United States, or that I was a resident of the State of Michigan on the twenty-fourth day of June, eighteen hundred and thirty-five, or that I was a resident of this State on the first day of January, eighteen hundred and fifty, and have declared my intentions to become a citizen of the United States pursuant to the laws thereof six months preceding this election, or that I have resided in this State two years and six months, and declared my intentions as aforesaid; that I am of the age of twenty-one years; that I am now, and for ten days last past have been, a resident of the City of Ann Arbor, and of the ward in which I now offer my vote, and that I have not voted at this election." Upon taking such oath, he shall forthwith be permitted to vote.

Sec. 10. It shall be the duty of the Recorder, as soon as practicable, and within five days after any election, to notify the officers respectively of their election, who shall, within ten days after receiving such notice, take an oath or affirmation to support the Constitution of the State of Michigan, and faithfully and impartially to perform the duties of their respective offices; a certificate of which oath, made by the person administering the same, shall be filed in the office of the Recorder.

Sec. 11. The Mayor, Recorder and Aldermen, when assembled together and organized, shall constitute the Common Council of the City of Ann Arbor, and a majority of the whole (the Mayor or Recorder always being one) shall be necessary to constitute a quorum for the transaction of business (but a less number may adjourn from time to time,) and the Common Council may be summoned to hold their meetings at such time as the Mayor, or in case of his absence or inability to act, the Recorder, may appoint, and at such place as shall have been designated as a council room by the Common Council. The Common Council shall have power to impose, levy and collect such fines as they may deem proper, not exceeding five dollars, for the non-attendance, at any meeting, of any officer of the corporation who has been duly notified to attend the same. The Mayor shall preside at all meetings of the Common Council, and the Recorder shall keep a record of the proceedings thereof. In case of the absence of the Mayor or Recorder from any such meeting, the members present may appoint a President or Recorder pro tempore.

Sec. 12. The Common Council shall have power to appoint an Attorney for the City, and a Chief Engineer of the Fire Department, and such other officers whose election is not herein specifically provided for, as they deem necessary to carry into effect the powers granted by this act, and to remove the same at pleasure. They shall also have power to remove the Marshal, Treasurer, or Street Commissioner, for any violation of the ordinances of the Common Council; and in case of the death, resignation, or removal from office, or neglect to qualify, of any officer of the corporation, the Common Council shall, as soon as may be, appoint an officer to fill such vacancy for the unexpired portion of the year, and all officers so appointed shall be notified and qualified as herein directed: *Provided*, That the Common Council may at any time order a special election to fill a vacancy in any office which is elective under this act.

Sec. 13. The Common Council shall have power to organize, maintain and regulate a Police of the City, and to make all such by-laws and ordinances as they shall deem necessary for the preservation of the public peace, for the suppression of riots, for the apprehension and punishment of vagrants, drunkards and disorderly persons, to suppress all disorderly houses and houses of ill-fame, to prohibit every species of gaming, for the prevention and abatement of all nuisances within the limits of the City, to prevent the selling or giving away of any spirituous or fermented liquors to any common drunkard, to regulate the keeping of gunpowder, and to prevent the discharge of every species of fire-arms, to prevent the violation of the Sabbath, and the disturbance of any religious congregation, or any other public meeting assembled for any lawful purpose, to provide against and punish immoderate riding or driving in any of the streets of the City; and for the purpose of carrying into effect the powers conferred by this section, the Common Council shall have power to prescribe in any by-law or ordinance which may be made by them, that the person offending against the same shall forfeit and pay such fine as they shall deem proper, not exceeding one hundred dollars, or be imprisoned in the county jail for a term not exceeding thirty days; or the Common Council may, in such by-law or ordinance, direct that the offender shall be punished by fine and imprisonment, or by both fine and imprisonment (within the limits aforesaid) in the discretion of the Justice who shall try the offender.

Sec. 14. Any Justice of the Peace residing in said City of Ann Arbor, shall have full power and authority, and it is hereby made the duty of such Justice, upon complaint to him in writing, to inquire into, and try and determine, all offences which shall be committed within said City against any of the by-laws or ordinances which shall be made by the Common Council in pursuance of the powers granted by this act ; and to punish the offenders as by the said by-laws or ordinances shall be prescribed or directed ; to award all process, and take recognizance for the keeping of the peace, for the appearance of the person charged, and upon appeal, and to commit to prison, as occasion shall lawfully require.

Sec. 15. The Corporation of the City of Ann Arbor shall be allowed to use the common jail of the county of Washtenaw for the imprisonment of all persons liable to imprisonment under the by-laws and ordinances of the Common Council ; and all persons committed to jail by any Justice of the Peace for any violation of a by-law or ordinance of said Common Council, shall be in the custody of the sheriff of the county, who shall safely keep the person so committed until lawfully discharged as in other cases.

Sec. 16. Whenever any person shall be charged with having violated any ordinance of the Common Council, by which the offender is liable to imprisonment, any Justice of the Peace residing in said City to whom complaint shall be made in writing and on oath, shall issue a warrant, directed to the Sheriff or any Constable of the County of Washtenaw, commanding him forthwith to bring the body of such person before him to be dealt with according to law, and the Marshal or other officer to whom said warrant shall be delivered for service, is hereby required to execute the same in any part of this State where such offender may be found, under the penalties which are by law incurred by Sheriffs and other officers for neglecting or refusing to execute other criminal process.

Sec. 17. All process issued by any Justice of the Peace to enforce or carry into effect any of the by-laws or ordinances of the Common Council, shall be directed to the Marshal of the City of Ann Arbor, or to the Sheriff or any Constable of the County of Washtenaw, and such process may be executed by any of said officers anywhere within this State, and shall be returned the same as other similar process issued by Justices of the Peace. The expenses of apprehending, examining and committing offenders against any law of this State in the said City, and of their confinement, shall be audited, allowed and paid by the Supervisors of the County of Washtenaw in the same manner as if such expenses had been incurred in any town of said county.

Sec. 18. The Mayor of said City shall have the same power, as conservator of the peace, within the limits of the City, as any Justice of the Peace has, or may by law have; and it is hereby made his duty to see that the by-laws and ordinances are faithfully enforced; and to this end it shall be lawful for him, when any person or persons shall in his presence be guilty of a breach of the peace, or any violation of an ordinance of the Common Council, punishable by imprisonment, to direct the Marshal or other officer forthwith to apprehend such offender or offenders and take him or them before a Justice of the Peace for said City, who shall, without unreasonable delay, proceed to the examination and trial of the party accused.

Sec. 19. The Marshal of said City shall, before entering upon the discharge of the duties of his office, give such security for the faithful performance of his duties as the Common Council shall direct and require. He shall be Chief of the Police, and it shall be his duty to serve all process that may be lawfully delivered to him for service; to see that all the by-laws and ordinances of the Common Council are promptly and efficiently enforced, and especially those which may be passed to carry into effect the powers granted by section thirteen of this act. He shall obey all the lawful orders of the Mayor, and may command the aid and assistance of all constables, and all other persons, in discharge of the duties imposed upon him by law. He may appoint such number of deputies as the Common Council shall direct and approve, who shall have the same powers and perform the same duties as the Marshal, and for whose official acts he shall be in all respects responsible; and the Marshal and his deputies shall have the same power to serve and execute all process on behalf of the corporation of said city, or of the people of this State, as sheriffs or constables have by law to execute similar process.

Sec. 20. The Common Council shall have power to make all such by-laws and ordinances as they shall deem necessary and proper to secure said City and the inhabitants thereof against injuries by fire; to compel the owners or occupants of buildings to procure and keep in readiness such number of fire buckets as they may direct; to establish, maintain and regulate all such fire engine, hook and ladder, and hose and bucket companies as they may deem expedient; to construct reservoirs, and provide such companies with necessary and proper buildings, engines and other implements to prevent and extinguish fires ; to appoint from among the inhabitants of said City such number of persons, not exceeding eighty to any one company, as are willing to accept or as may be deemed proper to be employed as firemen ; and every such company shall have power to appoint its own officers, and to pass by-laws for its organization and government, subject to the approval of the Common Council, and to impose and collect such fines for non-attendance or neglect of duty of its members as may be deemed necessary and proper ; and every person belonging to such company shall annually obtain from the Recorder a certificate, which shall be prima facie evidence of his membership for one year from the date thereof. Every member of such company during his membership shall be exempt from service on juries, from military duty in time of peace, and from the payment of a poll tax.

Sec. 21. It shall be the duty of such company to keep in good order and repair its fire engine, hose, ladders, and other implements ; to assemble at least once in each month for the purpose of working its fire engine ; and upon any alarm, or breaking out of fire within said City, each company shall forthwith assemble at the place of such fire, with its fire engine and other implements, and be subject to the orders of the Chief Engineer of the Fire Department.

Sec. 22. Upon the breaking out of any fire in said City, the Marshal shall immediately repair to the place of such fire, and aid and assist, as well in extinguishing the fire, as in preventing any goods or property from being stolen or injured, and in protecting, removing and securing the same: for which purpose, and as Chief of the Police, he may require the assistance of all bystanders ; and in the performance of his said duties, the Marshal shall in all respects be subject to the orders of the Mayor, or such of the Aldermen as may be present.

Sec. 23. The Common Council shall have power, and it shall be their duty, to adopt measures for the preservation of the public health of said City; to restrain or prohibit the exercise of any unwholesome or dangerous avocation within the limits of the City; to establish a Board of Health, and to invest it with such powers, and to impose upon it such duties, as shall be necessary to secure the inhabitants of said City from contagious, malignant and infectious diseases; to provide for its proper organization, and for the appointment of the proper officers; and they shall have authority to make all such by-laws and regulations for the grovernment of such Board of Health, and for the preservation of the health of the inhabitants of said City, as shall secure a prompt and efficient discharge of the duties imposed upon the Common Council by this act.

Sec. 24. The Common Council shall have power to regulate the time and manner of working upon the streets, lanes and alleys of said City; to provide for the grading, planking or paving, and and railing the sidewalks, and to prescribe the width thereof; to prevent the obstruction or encumbering of any of the streets, lanes, alleys, sidewalks or public grounds in said City; to provide for the erection and maintenance of lamp posts and lamps in said streets, and to provide for the lighting of the same; to provide for the planting and protection of shade trees along the sides of the streets and on the public grounds in said City, and to keep such public grounds in good condition; to lay out, open, make and repair streets and alleys, and the same to alter and vacate, and to alter or vacate those already laid out. Before any street, lane or alley shall be laid out, altered or vacated, the Common Council shall give notice thereof to the owners, occupants, or persons interested, or his or their agent or representative, by personal service, or by posting up notices in five or more public places in the City, stating the time and place when and where the Common Council will meet to consider the same, and describing the street, lane or alley proposed to be laid out, altered or vacated—which notice shall be posted at least ten days before the time of meeting. If, after hearing the persons interested who may appear before them, the Common Council shall determine to lay out or alter any street, lane or alley, they may purchase of any person or persons through whose lands the same may pass, the right of way. If the sum to be paid therefor shall not be agreed upon, it shall be lawful for the Mayor, or in case the Mayor shall be absent, for the Recorder, to apply to any Justice of the Peace of said City for the appointment of a jury of twelve freeholders of the county to ascertain the necessity of taking the property described in such application, and to appraise the damage thereon to such person or persons as shall not have released all claim for damages or agreed with the Common Council on the price to be paid by reason of the laying out or altering such street, lane or alley—which application shall describe the premises through which it is proposed to alter or lay out such street, lane or alley. Upon the receipt of such application, said Justice shall make a list of twelve disinterested freeholders residing in the county, and shall issue a venirie under his hand, directed to the Marshal of said City or any constable of said county, commanding to summon the persons named in said list to be and appear at his office on some day to be therein named, not less than six days nor more than twelve days from the time of issuing the same, to serve as jurors to ascertain the necessity of taking the property described in such application for the purposes of such street, lane or alley, and to appraise the damage thereon; and if all the jurors shall not appear, the said Justice shall cause a sufficient number of talesmen to be summoned to make a full jury. The jurors shall be sworn by such Justice to ascertain the necessity of taking the property described in the application, and justly and impartially to appraise the damage thereon. They shall then proceed to view the premises described, and shall within five days thereafter make return to the said Justice in writing, signed by them, of their doings, which shall state if such street, lane or alley be laid out, the necessity of taking the property described in such application, the amount of damages appraised, if any, to whom payable if known, and a statement of the time spent by them for that purpose—which return shall be certified by said Justice, and filed in the Recorder's office. Such jurors shall be entitled to receive one dollar per day and fifty cents for each half day, and the

Justice and Constable each one dollar for their fees, and the damages which shall be assessed as hereinbefore, or which shall have been contended [contracted] to be paid by said Common Council as in this section provided, and the fees and charges lawfully incurred, shall be levied and collected in said City, and shall be paid on the order of the Common Council as other city charges. The Mayor or Recorder may, instead of procuring the summoning of a jury as hereinbefore provided, make application to a court of record for the appointment of three commissioners, whose duty it shall be to ascertain and determine the necessity of taking the property described in such application, and in case of such application the same proceedings shall be had, and said court and commissioners shall have the same powers and shall be entitled to the same fees as are provided in act number thirteen of the session laws of eighteen hundred and fifty eight, approved February third, eighteen hundred and fifty eight. All sums so assessed shall be paid or tendered to the person or persons in favor of whom such assessment shall be made, before such street, lane or alley shall be opened or used. If any person in whose favor such assessment shall be made shall refuse to receive the amount of such assessment, or if he shall not reside in said City so that the same can be tendered to him, the money shall be deposited with the Treasurer of the City to be delivered to the person lawfully entitled to receive the same, and thereupon the Common Council may proceed forthwith to cause such street, lane or alley to be opened and used: *Provided*, That any person claiming damages who shall be aggrieved by such assessment, may appeal therefrom to the Circuit Court of the County of Washtenaw, and upon giving written notice to the Mayor of his intention to appeal within five days after the assessment shall be made; but such appeal shall not prevent the immediate opening or altering and using of such street, lane or alley. Upon filing a copy of said assessment, with a copy of the notice of appeal in the said Circuit Court at its next session, or within ten days after such assessment is made, the Court shall have jurisdiction of the appeal, and shall proceed in the same manner as is usual in other cases of appeal, to assess the damages, and if the damages awarded by the Court upon such appeal shall not be greater than the damages assessed by the jury, or shall have been tendered or deposited as hereinbefore provided, the Court shall give judgment against the party appealing for the costs of the appeal.

Sec. 25. The Street Commissioner, and such other officer as the Common Council shall direct and appoint, shall, under the direction of the Common Council, superintend the making, paving, repairing and opening of all streets, lanes, alleys, bridges and sidewalks within the limits of the City, in such manner as he or they may from time to time be directed. The Common Council shall have power to cause the expenses of making, paving and opening streets, lanes and alleys, of grading, paving or planking sidewalks, of making drains and sewers, and other local improvements, to be assessed against the owners or occupants of the lots or premises which are in front of or adjoining such improvements, or by general tax, as they may deem just and proper : *Provided*, That no such assessment shall be made or collected other than by general tax, unless upon the application, in writing, of two-thirds of all the resident owners or occupants of the real estate which may be subject to pay the tax for such local improvement. And the Common Council shall have power to make all by-laws and ordinances relative to the mode of assessing, levying and collecting such tax, and they may by such by-laws and ordinances provide that the real estate assessed for such improvements may be sold or leased for a term of years to pay such assessment.

Sec. 26. The Common Council shall have authority to make all by-laws and ordinances relative to the powers, duties and compensation of the officers of said corporation, subject to the restrictions as to the compensation of officers mentioned in this act ; relative to the calling of meetings of the electors of the City; to licensing showmen and other exhibitions where money or other consideration is demanded or received for admission, and to fix the amount of such license ; to protect and regulate all public grave yards, and the burial of the dead in said City ; to direct the number of, and license inkeepers and common victualers ; to provide for the collection and disposition of all fines and penalties which may be incurred under the by-laws and ordinances of said City ; to prevent swine, cattle, horses, dogs and other animals from running at large in said

City, and to establish and regulate one or more pounds therein, and to make all such other by-laws, ordinances and regulations for the purpose of carrying into effect the powers conferred by this act which they may deem necessary to provide for the safety and good government of the City, and preserve the health and protect the property of the inhabitants thereof ; and to this end, the Common Council may impose fines and penalties for any violation of the by-laws and ordinances which may be made by them as aforesaid : *Provided*, That no by-law or ordinance shall impose a fine exceeding one hundred dollars, nor subject the offender to imprisonment in the county jail exceeding thirty days : **and** *Provided further*, That no by-law or ordinance of the Common Council, subjecting any person to fine or imprisonment, shall be of any effect until the same shall have been published for two weeks successively in a newspaper printed in said City.

SEC. 27. All fines imposed by any by-law or ordinance of the Common Council, may be sued for by the Attorney of the City, in his own name or in the name of the corporation, before any Justice of the Peace of said City ; and whenever any fine shall be imposed by any Justice of the Peace for a violation of any ordinance of the Common Council, it shall be the duty of the Justice forthwith to issue execution to the Marshal of the City, commanding him to collect of the goods and chattels of the person so offending, the amount of such fine, with interest and costs ; and for the want of goods and chattels wherewith to satisfy the same, that he take the body of the defendant and commit him to the common jail of the county, and the Sheriff shall safely keep the body of the person so committed until he be discharged by due course of law ; and the defendant shall remain imprisoned until the execution, with the fees of the Sheriff, shall be paid : *Provided*, That the Common Council may remit such fine, in whole or in part, if it shall be made to appear that the person so imprisoned is unable to pay the same.

SEC. 28. All actions against the City of Ann Arbor shall be commenced by summons, which shall be served upon the Recorder at least six days before the return day thereof, by giving him a copy of said summons, with the name of the officer serving the same endorsed thereon ; or in ease of the absence of the Recorder from the City, then by leaving such copy with the Mayor, endorsed as aforesaid.

Sec. 29. In all suits in which the corporation of the City of Ann Arbor shall be a party, or shall be interested, no inhabitant of said City shall be deemed incompetent as a witness or juror, on account of his interest in the event of such suit or action : *Provided*, Such interest be such only as he has in common with the inhabitants of said City.

Sec. 30. In all trials before any Justice of the Peace, of any person charged with a violation of any by-law or ordinance of the Common Council, either party shall be entitled to a jury of six persons, and all the proceedings for the summoning of such jury, and in the trial of the cause, shall be in conformity, as near as may be, with the mode of proceeding in similar cases before Justices of the Peace ; and in all cases, civil and criminal, the right of appeal from the justice's court to the county or circuit court having jurisdiction of the cause, shall be allowed ; and the party appealing shall enter into a recognizance, conditioned to prosecute the appeal in the county or circuit court, as the case may be, and abide the order of the court therein, or such other recognizance as is or may be required by law in appeals from justice's courts in similar cases.

Sec. 31. The Common Council shall have power to assess and collect, from every white male inhabitant of said City, over the age of twenty-one years, (except paupers, idiots, and lunatics,) an annual capitation or poll tax, not exceeding seventy-five cents ; and they may provide by their by-laws for the collection of the same : *Provided*, That any person assessed for a poll tax may pay the same by one day's labor upon the streets under the direction of the Street Commissioner, who shall give to each person so assessed, notice of the time and place when and where such labor will be required; and the money raised by such poll tax, or the labor in lieu thereof, shall be expended or performed in the respective wards where the persons so taxed shall reside.

Sec. 32. The Common Council of said City is hereby authorized and required to perform the same duties in and for said City as are by-law imposed upon the township boards of the several townships of this State, in reference to schools, school taxes, county and state taxes, the support of the poor, and state, district, and county elections; and the Supervisor and Assessor, Justices of the Peace, Recorder, School Inspectors, Directors of the Poor, and all other officers of said City who are required to perform the duties of township officers of this State, shall take the oath, give the bond, perform like duties, and receive the same pay and in the same manner, and be subject to the same liabilities, as is provided for the corresponding township officers, excepting as is otherwise provided in this act, or as may be provided by the ordinances of the Common Council.

Sec. 33. The Common Council shall have authority to assess, levy and collect taxes on all the real and personal estate taxable in said City, which taxes shall be and remain a lien upon the property so assessed, until the same shall be paid: *Provided*, That they shall not raise, by general tax, in any one year, exclusive of school taxes, more than one thousand and five hundred dollars for general purposes, nor more than two thousand dollars for street or highway purposes, unless authorized thereto by a vote of the property tax-payers of said City, who are electors, when convened for that purpose pursuant to previous notice.

Sec. 34 Whenever the Common Council shall deem it necessary to raise a greater sum in any one year, exclusive of school taxes, than one thousand and five hundred dollars for general purposes, or two thousand dollars for street or highway purposes, they shall give at least five days' notice, in writing, to be posted up in five public places in said City—which notice shall state the time and place of such meeting, and shall specify the objects and purposes for which the money proposed to be raised is to be expended, and when such meeting shall be assembled in pursuance of such notice, such electors, by a *viva voce* vote, shall determine the amount of money which shall be raised for each object specified in the notice: *Provided*, That such tax shall not in any one year exceed one per cent on the valuation of the real and personal estate taxable within the limits of the City: and *Provided also*, That not more than two such meetings shall be holden in any one year to determine the amount of tax to be raised. At all such meetings the Mayor, or in his absence the Recorder, shall preside.

Sec. 35. The Common Council may appoint the Alderman to assist the Supervisor in taking the assessment of property in the respective wards where the Alderman resides; and all state, county and school taxes in said City, and all City taxes which shall be raised by general tax, shall be levied and collected, as near as may be, in the same manner as is provided by law for the assessment and collection of taxes by township officers; and all proceedings for the return, sale, and redemption of real estate for non-payment of taxes shall be in conformity with the proceedings for the return, sale, and redemption of real estate by township officers.

Sec. 36. Whenever the Common Council shall be authorized by a vote of the property tax-payers of said City to raise a tax for any specific purpose, and which cannot be included in the assessment roll and collected or returned for non-payment as provided in section thirty-five of this act, it shall be lawful for the Common Council to apportion such tax upon the property according to the valuation as contained in the then last City assessment roll, and shall place the tax in a column opposite the valuation of the property, and when such roll is completed, the Recorder shall make and deliver a copy thereof to the City Treasurer, together with a warrant signed by the Mayor and Recorder, commanding the Treasurer to collect the same, and make return of his proceedings by virtue of said warrant within a time in said warrant to be specified, not less than thirty nor more than ninety days from the date thereof; and it shall be the duty of the Treasurer to collect said taxes within the time specified in said warrant, or within such further time as the Common Council may by resolution direct.

Sec. 37. The Common Council may by ordinance provide for the collection of all taxes necessary to be raised, other than such as may be raised as provided in section thirty-five, and for the sale of any real estate for the non-payment of such tax, and for the redemption thereof: *Provided*, That all the proceedings relative to the notice of sale, the manner of conducting the same, and the time to redeem, shall be in conformity, as near as may be, to the provisions of law regulating the sale of lands delinquent for township taxes.

Sec. 38. The Treasurer of said City shall keep a regular account of all moneys received and disbursed by him, in books to be previded for that purpose, in which the name of every person to whom money shall be paid, shall be entered at full length, and on what account the same was paid; which books shall at all reasonable hours be open to the inspection of any freeman of said City. All moneys received for the use of said City shall be paid into the City treasury; and no money shall be drawn from the treasury unless it shall have been previously appropriated by the Common Council to the purpose for which it shall be drawn; and the Treasurer shall pay out no money but upon the written warrant of the Mayor and Recorder.

SEC. 39. No bond, note, or other obligation or evidence of indebtedness of said corporation, except orders on the Treasurer as hereinafter provided, shall ever be given or issued by said corporation or by any officer thereof in his official capacity, whereby the said City shall become obligated to pay any sum of money; but the Common Council may allow just claims against the City, and may issue orders therefor on the Treasurer payable on the first day of February next thereafter, but such orders shall not in the aggregate in any one year, exceed the aggregate of taxes levied to pay the same in such year.

SEC. 40. The officers of said corporation shall be entitled to receive, out of the City treasury, the following sums in full payment for their services: The Mayor shall be paid one dollar per annum; the Aldermen shall be entitled to receive one dollar per day when employed in assisting the Supervisor in taking the assessment; the Recorder and Attorney shall be entitled to receive respectively such sum as the Common Council shall allow, not exceeding one hundred dollars per annum; the Marshal shall be entitled to receive the same fees for serving process in behalf of the corporation as constables are by law allowed for similar services, and he shall also receive such further compensation, not exceeding one hundred dollars per annum, as the Common Council shall allow; the Treasurer and Collector, Justices of the Peace and Constables, shall be allowed the same fees as are by law allowed to corresponding township officers; the Street Commissioner, Supervisors, Directors of the Poor, School Inspectors, and all other officers of said City, shall be entitled to receive such compensation as the Common Council shall allow, not exceeding one dollar and a half per day for every day actually employed in the performance of the duties of their respective offices.

Sec. 41. The Common Council shall, in the month of March in each year, make out a detailed statement of all the receipts and expenditures of the corporation for the past year, which statement shall state particularly upon what account all moneys were received, and it shall also specify all appropriations made by the Common Council during the year, and the particular purpose for which each appropriation was made. Such statement shall be signed by the Mayor and Recorder, and be filed in the Recorder's office, and a copy thereof shall be published in a newspaper printed in said City for at least two weeks.

Sec. 42. All the rights of the corporation known as the Common Council of the Village of Ann Arbor in and to all personal and real estate, rights, credits and effects whatsoever, is hereby declared to be fully and absolutely vested in the corporation created by this act, saving nevertheless to all and every person his or their just rights therein; and to the end that all and singular the estates, rights and property aforesaid may be fully vested in the corporation of the City of Ann Arbor, every person who is or shall be possessed thereof, shall deliver the same to the Mayor, Recorder and Aldermen, with all moneys, deeds, evidences of debt, property, books and papers touching or concerning the same, when legally required thereto.

Sec. 43. The Township of Ann Arbor shall retain its present organization, subject to the alteration of boundaries herein made and provided, and the next annual township meeting for said township shall be held at the Washtenaw House, at which election there shall be chosen all such township officers as by law the several townships are authorized to elect. The electors at such election may choose the judges and clerk thereof, and all the provisions of law relative to the adjournment of the place of holding such election shall apply to such meeting.

Sec. 44. All acts heretofore enacted in regard to the Village of Ann Arbor, coming within the perview of this act, are hereby repealed: *Provided, That* the repealing of said act shall not effect any act already done, or any right acquired under, or proceeding had or commenced by virtue thereof, but the same shall remain as valid as if said acts remained in full force.

SEC. 45. This act shall be deemed a public act, and shall be favorably construed in all courts.

SEC. 46. The Legislature may at any time alter, amend or repeal this act.

SEC. 47. This act shall take effect and be in force from and after its passage.

Original Act approved April 4, 1851,

Amendatory Act approved February 12, 1858.

An ACT to extend the limits and jurisdiction of the City of Ann Arbor, in relation to Burying Grounds.

SECTION 1. *The People of the State of Michigan enact,* That all that part of the west half of the south-east quarter of section number twenty-eight, in township number two south of range number six east, lying northerly of the center line of the Geddes road in the township of Ann Arbor, be set off and taken from the township of Ann Arbor, and added to, and made a part of the City of Ann Arbor, in the county of Washtenaw, and that the district so added to said City shall hereafter be subject to all laws, ordinances and regulations which shall at any time be in force in said City, and cease to be subject to the regulations or government of the township of Ann Arbor; and the Common Council of the City of Ann Arbor shall have power and authority to make such by-laws or ordinances, and prescribe such rules and regulations as they may deem necessary and expedient for the protection, management and government of any Cemetery or Burial Ground that is or may be on the above described land, or elsewhere in said City, and to prescribe in and by any such by-laws or ordinances, that any person or persons violating any of the by-laws, ordinances, rules or regulations so made;

shall or may, upon conviction thereof, be punished by a fine not exceeding twenty-five dollars, or by imprisonment in the county jail not exceeding thirty days, or by both, in the discretion of the court or justice before whom the offender shall be tried.

Ordered to take immediate effect.

Approved February 5, 1859.

ORDINANCES.

No. 1.

AN ORDINANCE TO PREVENT HOGS FROM RUNNING AT LARGE.

Be it Ordained by the Mayor, Recorder and Aldermen of the City of Ann Arbor—

SECTION 1. That it shall not be lawful for any swine, hogs, shoats or pigs to go at large within the limits of the City of Ann Arbor; and if any swine, hogs, shoats or pigs shall be found running at large within the limits of said City, it shall be lawful for any person, and it shall be the duty of the Marshal of said City, to drive the same to pound within said City, or cause the same to be so driven; and for driving the same to pound as aforesaid, the Marshal, or any person employed for that purpose by him, shall be entitled to receive the sum of ten cents for each hog, shoat or pig so driven to pound.

Sec. 2. It shall be the duty of the Marshal to provide a suitable pound within said City for all such animals as may be driven to pound under the provisions of any ordinance of the Common Council, and to receive and safely keep such animals therein until the provisions of the ordinance under which they were impounded shall have been complied with. And it shall be lawful for said Marshal to demand and receive as his fee for taking in and discharging every hog, shoat or pig, six cents; which fee, together with the fees of driving such animals to pound, and the reasonable charges for keeping and feeding the same therein, not exceeding twelve and a half cents per day for each animal, shall be paid to the Marshal by the owner thereof, or some other person for him, before such animal shall be released from said pound, and if the owner of any such animal impounded as aforesaid shall not pay the fees for impounding, and the reasonable charges for keeping the same, within two days after the same were impounded, then it shall and may be lawful for said Marshal to sell such animals at public vendue, giving at least two days previous notice thereof by advertisement posted up at such pound and the nearest public house thereto, and from the moneys accruing from such sale to retain the fees for impounding and keeping such animal, together with ten per cent upon the avails of such sale for advertising and selling such animal, and to return the surplus to the owner of such animal; and if no owner shall appear within six months after such sale, the same shall be paid to the Treasurer of said City.

Sec. 3. It shall be the duty of the Marshal to carry the provisions of this ordinance into full effect; and upon complaint and conviction before any Justice of the Peace in said City of a neglect or failure after due notice to drive to pound any hogs found running at large as aforesaid, or to impound any hog, shoat or pig driven to pound by any other person according to the provisions of this ordinance, he shall be sentenced to pay a fine of one dollar for each neglect, together with costs of prosecution,

Sec. 4. If any person shall hereafter wilfully break or attempt to break any pound which may hereafter be erected or provided in said City, or rescue, or attempt to rescue any animal confined therein, or while being driven thereto under any ordinance of the Common Council, he shall, upon conviction thereof before any Justice of the Peace of said City, be fined in a sum not exceeding fifty dollars and costs of prosecution.

Sec. 5. This ordinance shall take effect and be in force from and after the 20th day of May instant.

Made and passed in Common Council at the City of Ann Arbor this 6th day of May, 1851.

GEO. SEDGWICK, Mayor.

E. W. MORGAN, Recorder pro tem.

No. 2.

AN ORDINANCE RELATIVE TO STUD HORSES.

Be it Ordained by the Mayor, Recorder and Aldermen of the City of Ann Arbor—

That from and after the passage of this ordinance it shall not be lawful for any person to display or detain for public exhibition, or for the purposes of generation in the City of Ann Arbor, any stud horse; any person so offending shall be liable to a fine of five dollars and costs, to be recovered in an action of debt, before any Justice of the Peace of said City.

Made and passed in Common Council at the City of Ann Arbor this 6th day of May, 1851.

GEO. SEDGWICK, Mayor.

E. W. MORGAN, Recorder pro tem.

No. 3.

AN ORDINANCE RELATIVE TO THE FIRE DEPARTMENT OF THE CITY OF ANN ARBOR.

Be it Ordained by the Mayor, Recorder and Aldermen of the City of Ann Arbor—

SECTION 1. The Fire Department of the City of Ann Arbor shall consist of a Chief Engineer, an Assistant Engineer, one Fire Warden in each Ward, and so many Fire Engine, Hook and Ladder, Hose and Bucket companies as the Common Council shall from time to time direct. The Chief and Assistant Engineers and Fire Wardens shall be appointed by the Common Council annually in the month of May, or as soon thereafter as may be, and shall hold their offices until the first day of May next ensuing their election, and until their successors are appointed.

Sec. 2. The Chief Engineer shall have full power, control and command over all persons whatever, at any fire, except members of the Common Council; and in his absence the Assistant Engineer shall perform his duties. In the absence of the Chief and Assistant Engineers from any fire, the Mayor, and in his absence the Recorder, shall discharge the duties of Chief Engineer until the proper officer shall arrive and assume the command.

Sec. 3. It shall be the duty of the Chief Engineer at all fires, to direct such measures as he may deem most proper for the speedy extinguishment of the fire. He shall also have the general supervision of the fire engines and other apparatus and property belonging to the Fire Department, and shall from time to time ascertain and report to the Common Council the repairs necessary to be made to keep the engines, hose, apparatus and property of the Fire Department in good repair and serviceable order. He shall also, as often as once in six months, report to the Common Council all accidents by fire that may happen in the City, with the cause thereof as near as can be ascertained, with the number and description of buildings destroyed or injured, and the names of the owners or occupants thereof, and the estimated loss of property at each fire.

Sec. 4. At every fire, each Fire Warden shall report himself to the Chief Engineer or other officer in command, and shall be subject to his orders. It shall be the duty of the Fire Wardens at every fire to protect the hose, buckets and other property of the Fire Department from injury; to keep all idle and suspected persons from the fire and its vicinity; to form lines for the conveyance of water to the engines, and for that purpose they shall have authority to command all persons present to form lines or otherwise aid in supplying the engine with water; and if any person shall refuse to obey such order of the wardens, he may be immediately expelled from the vicinity of the fire.

Sec. 5. Any person who shall at any fire wilfully resist, hinder or obstruct any officer or other person in the discharge of his duty at such fire, or who shall wilfully injure any hose or apparatus belonging to the fire department, may be arrested and detained in custody by any Fire Warden until such fire is extinguished; and such person shall for every such offence, forfeit and pay a fine of ten dollars, and be liable to an action for the recovery of damages.

Sec. 6. The Aldermen of said City shall ex-officio be fire wardens, and any member of the Common Council may, at all fires, exercise the same power and authority as is conferred upon the fire wardens by sections four and five of this ordinance.

Sec. 7. There shall be and hereby is established, one Fire Engine Company, to be known as "Eagle Fire Company No. 1, of the City of Ann Arbor;" which company shall be composed of not less than twenty, nor more than fifty members. The Fire Engine, Hose, apparatus and other property belonging to, or used by the present fire engine company in said City, is hereby transferred to, and shall be and remain under the charge and control of the fire engine company hereby established, until otherwise ordered by the Common Council.

Sec. 8. The officers of said company shall consist of a Foreman, a First and Second Assistant Foreman, four Wardens, a Secretary, Treasurer and Steward, and such other officers as the members thereof may see fit to elect. The members of said company shall elect their own officers at such time and in such manner as they shall think proper. They may adopt a constitution and pass by-laws for the government of the company, subject to the approval of the Common Council, and may impose and collect such fines for the non-attendance or neglect of duty of any member of the company as they may deem necessary and proper.

Sec. 9. It shall be the duty of every member of any fire company which is or may be formed in said City, upon the breaking out of any fire in said City, to repair immediately upon the alarm thereof to their respective fire apparatus, and convey the same to the place where such fire shall happen, and under the direction of the Chief Engineer and their several officers to work and manage their engines and apparatus belonging thereto, for the extinguishment of the fire, and not remove therefrom but by the direction of the Chief Engineer, or other officer authorized to direct them, which direction being obtained they shall return with their engines and implements to their several places of deposit, and as soon thereafter as may be, wash and clean the same.

Sec. 10. It shall be the duty of the Foreman of every company belonging to the Fire Department to return to the Common Council the names of all the persons composing such company, stating the times when they severally became such members; and when any person shall for any reason have ceased to be a member, the Foreman shall certify that fact to the Common Council, and any person whose name shall be returned by the Foreman as a member of any company may apply to the Recorder annually and obtain a certificate of his membership, which shall for one year thereafter be prima facie evidence of his membership and shall exempt him from service on juries, from military duty in time of peace, and from the payment of a poll tax.

3

Sec. 11. It shall be lawful for the Chief Engineer, or Assistant Engineer, or the Foreman or Assistant Foreman, or any Fire Warden or member of the Common Council to require the aid of any inhabitant of said City in drawing any fire engine or other apparatus of the Fire Department to any fire, or to require the aid of any bystander at the fire to work any engine or apparatus at the same, and on neglect or refusal to comply with such requisition without sufficient excuse, such person may be forthwith removed from the vicinity of the fire, or he may be arrested and detained in custody until the fire shall be extinguished, and shall be liable to a penalty not exceeding ten dollars.

Sec. 12. The Marshal, Deputy Marshal, and every Constable in said City shall repair immediately on the alarm of fire to the place where such fire may be, and report himself to any member of the Common Council, and aid and assist as well in extinguishing the fire as in preventing any goods or property from being stolen or injured, and in protecting, removing, and securing the same; they shall also aid in the preservation of the public peace, and the arrest or removal of all idle and suspected persons; and if the Marshal or any Constable shall neglect or refuse to obey any lawful order of any member of the Common Council, or the Chief Engineer, or any other officer authorized to direct at any fire, he shall pay a fine not exceeding twenty dollars.

Sec. 13. Any hook and ladder company, or any persons present at a fire shall, under the direction of the Chief Engineer and two members of the Common Council, or in the absence of the Chief Engineer, then under the direction of the Assistant Engineer and two members of the Common Council, or in the absence of the Chief and Assistant Engineers, then under the direction of three members of the Common Council and of the Foreman of a fire company, cut or pull down and remove any building or other erection, for the purpose of checking the progress of the fire.

Made and passed in Common Council at the City of Ann Arbor this 17th day of June, 1851.

GEO. SEDGWICK, Mayor.

HENRY W. WELLES, Recorder.

No. 4.

AN ORDINANCE RELATIVE TO THE PREVENTION OF FIRES.

Be it Ordained by the Mayor, Recorder and Aldermen of the City of Ann Arbor—

SECTION 1. That the Fire Wardens of the respective wards shall examine into and correct any infraction of the ordinances made for the protection of the City from fires in their respective wards particularly, and the City generally, and shall make reports to the Common Council respecting danger from exposure to fires on the first Mondays in June and December in each year; and any neglect of such duty shall subject the Fire Warden to a fine of five dollars, and to removal from office.

Sec. 2. It shall be the duty of the Fire Wardens or any two of them, twice in each year, in the months of May and November, and as much oftener as they may deem proper, between sunrise and sunset, to enter into any house or building, yard or premises in the City and examine the fire-places, chimneys, stoves and pipes thereto, and other apparatus likely to cause fires; also places where ashes, hay, straw, shavings or other combustible materials may be lodged, and to give such directions in regard thereto to the owner or occupant of such premises either for the removal, alteration or better care and management thereof as they may deem necessary to protect the City from fire; and such directions shall be complied with by the person or persons to whom they shall be given, and at the expense of such owner or occupant.

Sec. 3. The said Wardens shall have authority to cause chimneys to be burned out or otherwise cleaned, whenever they shall think it necessary—to require chimneys in blacksmiths' shops and furnaces to be so constructed or altered as to prevent sparks from exposing buildings to fire, and to remove or abate, with the consent of the Mayor, Recorder, or any Alderman, (if the owner or occupant shall neglect to do so,) any cause from which immediate danger from fire may be apprehended, at the expense of the person or persons occasioning the same.

Sec. 4. No stove pipe shall be put up or kept up in any building in said City unless it pass into a chimney made of brick or stone; nor shall any person at any time set fire to any chimney for the purpose of cleaning the same, without previous consent of the Fire Warden of the proper ward; and every person violating the provisions of this section shall forfeit for every offence three dollars, and the further sum of one dollar for every twenty-four hours any such stove pipe shall remain so put up after notice of any Fire Warden to alter the same.

Sec. 5. Every chimney hereafter to be erected in said City shall be plastered with lime mortar on the inside thereof, under a penalty of twenty dollars, and a further penalty of five dollars for every ten days neglect to take down or alter the same after notice given by a Fire Warden for that purpose. It shall be the duty of the Fire Wardens to examine all chimneys when the same are being constructed, and if they are not in conformity with the requirements of this section, to make report thereof to the Common Council.

Sec. 6. It shall not be lawful for any person to keep, within the limits of this City, at any one time, in any one building and its appurtenances, a greater quantity of gunpowder than twenty-eight pounds, the same to be well secured in metal canisters with metal stoppers or covers, neither of which shall contain more than seven pounds of powder; and it shall be lawful for any member of the

Common Council, the Chief Engineer, or Fire Warden, to seize any powder kept contrary to the provisions of this section and convert the same as forfeited to the use of the Fire Department; and every person so offending shall forfeit the powder so unlawfully kept, and shall also forfeit and pay the sum of one dollar for every pound of powder so kept contrary to the true intent and meaning of this section, to be recovered with costs of suit: *Provided*, That the Common Council may authorize any person to keep a quantity of gunpowder not exceeding two hundred pounds weight, at any one place in said City, with such protection against fire as they shall think proper.

Sec. 7. No person shall fire or set off any squib, cracker, gunpowder or fire works, or fire any gun or other species of fire-arms within the limits of this City, unless by the written permission of the Mayor or two Aldermen; which permission shall limit the time of such firing, and shall be subject to be revoked at any time by the Common Council. And any person violating any provisions of this section shall forfeit and pay a penalty not exceeding five dollars for each offence.

Sec. 8. Every person firing a cannon within the limits of this City, unless by permission of the Mayor or two Aldermen, shall forfeit and pay a penalty not exceeding twenty-five dollars.

Sec. 9. It shall not be lawful for any person hereafter to erect or place any building, or any part of a building, on any part of any block fronting or cornering on the court house square, nor on any lot fronting on Main street or Detroit street between North street and William street in this City, unless such building or part of a building shall be constructed of stone or brick, with party or fire walls of the same material rising at least ten inches above the roof, if the same be covered with metal or slate, and if covered with wood, then at least two feet: *Provided*, That nothing contained in this section shall be construed as prohibiting the erection, within the limits aforesaid, of any building of wood which shall not be more than eight feet square, nor of any wood house for keeping and storing fire wood which shall not exceed twenty feet in length, twelve feet in width, and twelve feet in height; nor of any barn which shall not exceed twenty-four feet in length, sixteen feet in width, and twelve feet in height from the common surface of the ground to the top of the plates, with roofs not to exceed one quarter pitch; but such small building, woodhouse or barn shall not be made to front on any street, nor be less than thirty feet from the line thereof; nor shall more than one such woodhouse or barn be allowed on any one lot or premises occupied as one tenement. [*No barn, privy, hog-pen, slaughter-house, or any other building which shall be used or occupied for any purpose liable to prove detrimental to the public health, or a nuisance to the adjoining occupant or to the public, shall be built fronting on any of the public streets of said City, nor within thirty feet from the line thereof.]

Sec. 10. If any person shall erect or put up any building within

---

* The words enclosed in brackets embrace the amendment made by Ordinance No. 26, which is omitted in its order.

the limits specified in section nine of this ordinance contrary to the provisions thereof, the owner or owners, builder or builders thereof shall severally forfeit and pay a penalty not exceeding fifty dollars for each offence, and also a penalty of twenty dollars for each and every week such building shall remain after notice from any member of the Common Council or Fire Warden to remove or alter the same.

Sec. 11, It shall not be lawful for any person to erect or use any steam engine on any block in said City adjoining Main street, Huron street or Detroit street, or at any place within forty rods of the court house square, under a penalty of not exceeding fifty dollars for each offence, and ten dollars for each and every day the same shall be used: *Provided,* That nothing contained in this section shall apply to the using of any steam engine now set up for use in said City where the same is now used.

Made and passed in Common Council in the City of Ann Arbor, this 17th day of June, 1851.

GEO. SEDGWICK, Mayor.

HENRY W. WELLES, Recorder.

No. 5.

AN ORDINANCE RELATIVE TO NUISANCES.

Be it Ordained by the Mayor, Recorder and Aldermen of the City of Ann Arbor—

Sec. 1. If any person or persons within the boundaries of this City, shall permit or suffer any nuisance on his, her or their premises, of which he, she or they shall be occupants, either by exercising any unwholesome or offensive trade or calling, or by permitting any building. sewer or other thing whatsoever to remain on said premises, until by offensive or ill stenches or otherwise they or any of them shall become offensive, hurtful or dangerous to the neighborhood or to travelers, it shall be the duty of the Marshal to give notice to said person or persons to remove such nuisance forthwith; and if the owner or owners, occupant or occupants of the premises on which such nuisance shall be situate, shall neglect or refuse to remove the same for the space of twenty-four hours after such notice shall be given, he, she or they, on conviction thereof, shall be liable to pay a fine of five dollars for each day he, she or they shall have permitted such nuisance to remain after notice as aforesaid.

Sec. 2. No person shall throw, place or deposit, or suffer his servant, child or family to throw, place or deposit any dead animal, carrion, putrid meat or fish, entrails or decayed vegetables, or any filthy or offensive matter of any kind whatsoever, or any substance which by any process can become putrid or offensive, in the streets, lanes or alleys in said City; nor shall he expose the same in such manner as to render the air in the neighborhood impure, offensive or unhealthy upon his own premises, or the premises of another; and any person who shall violate the provisions of this section shall be liable to pay a fine not exceeding twenty-five dollars for each offence.

Sec. 3. It shall not be lawful for any person to throw or place the contents of any straw bed, or any ashes, shells of oysters or clams, or any scraps of dirt from any shoemaker's, tailor's, black-smith's or tinner's shop; or to place or throw any shavings, straw or rubbish of any kind in any of the streets, lanes, alleys or public grounds, or upon any side-walks in said City; and any person or persons wilfully violating the provisions of this section shall forfeit and pay a penalty of two dollars for every offence.

Sec. 4. It shall be the duty of the Marshal to require all persons guilty of the offences mentioned in the two preceding sections, to remove such offensive matter, and on their failing to do so, to cause the same to be removed at the expense of the corporation, and the guilty person shall be liable to the corporation for such expenses, in addition to the penalty above imposed.

Made and passed in Common Council, this 17th day of June, 1851.

GEO. SEDGWICK, Mayor.

HENRY W. WELLES, Recorder.

———

No. 6.

AN ORDINANCE RELATIVE TO SHOWS, THEATRICAL AND OTHER EXHIBITIONS.

Be it Ordained by the Mayor, Recorder and Aldermen of the City of Ann Arbor—

SECTION 1. It shall not be lawful for any person or persons to make or exhibit any show, or to perform or exhibit any plays, games, theatrical or other performances or exhibitions whatever, or to exhibit any natural or other curiosities for which pay in money or other consideration of any kind shall be demanded or received for admission, within the limits of the City of Ann Arbor, with-out having previously obtained a license so to do, as hereinafter provided.

Sec. 2. It shall be the duty of every person who may be desirous of exhibiting any such curiosities or shows, or of performing any plays, games, theatrical or other exhibition for which any conside-ration shall be demanded or received for admission, to make appli-cation to the Common Council, or to the Mayor and two Aldermen, or in the absence of the Mayor, to the Recorder and two Aldermen, for a license. and such license may be granted if deemed proper; upon payment into the city treasury of such sum as may be directed, and which shall be specified in such license.

Sec. 3. Any person or persons offending against the provisions of this ordinance shall be liable to a fine not exceeding one hundred dollars for every offence, and the Marshal of the City is hereby authorized and required in every case where the provisions of this ordinance shall be violated, to arrest the person or persons offending against the same when directed so to do by the officers authorized to grant a license, and bring him or them forthwith before such officers, who are hereby authorized to hold such persons to bail for their appearance before any Justice of the Peace of said City to answer to such alleged offence: *Provided*, That any such person or persons may be discharged by the officers authorized to grant a license upon payment of such sum as they may direct, with costs.

Made and passed in Common Council this 17th day of June, A. D. 1851.

GEO. SEDGWICK, Mayor.

HENRY W. WELLES, Recorder.

———

No. 7.

AN ORDINANCE RELATIVE TO SIDEWALKS.

Be it Ordained by the Mayor, Recorder and Aldermen of the City of Ann Arbor—

SECTION 1. The side-walks in the several streets in the City of Ann Arbor shall be and the same are hereby established of the following width, to wit: On the west side of Main street, between Ann and Washington streets, the side-walk shall be fourteen feet in width; on the east side of Main street, between Huron and Washington streets—on the north side of Ann street, between Main and Fourth streets—on the south side of Huron street, between Main and Fourth streets, and on the east side of Fourth street between Ann and Huron streets, the side-walks shall be respectively twelve feet in width, and in all the other streets in said City the sidewalks shall be ten feet in width.

Sec. 2. A space in front of the established line of all streets, not exceeding one-third the width of the side-walk in such street, as established by section one of this ordinance, shall be allowed for projections, and it shall not be lawful for any person to place or cause to be placed upon any side-walk, lying outside the line allowed for projections as aforesaid, any box, barrel, article of merchandize or other obstruction or incumbrance whatever, or suffer or permit any obstruction to a free passage over such side-walk to exist, by leaving open any passage-way to cellars, or otherwise, excepting so far as the same may be necessary and unavoidable in transporting articles across the side-walk.

Sec. 3. No person shall place, put up, erect or suspend, or suffer to remain placed, put up, erected or suspended from any building or upon any lot within the limits of this City, any sign, show board or show bill, which shall extend from the front of such building or lot over the side-walk more than three feet, nor shall such sign or show-board be less than eight feet in height above the side-walk.

Sec. 4. All posts or railings put up in any street for the support of awnings, shall be placed on the established line between the side-walk and street; nor shall any awning, or the rails or boards used for connecting the awning-posts with the buildings, be less than eight feet in height above the side-walk.

Sec. 5. And to the end that there shall be and remain a free passage for all persons over and across the side-walks of the City, for at least two-thirds the established width thereof from the outer line of the street, free from all obstructions thereon, or passage ways to cellars, or awnings or rails less than eight feet in height above the side-walk, it shall be the duty of the Marshal, upon knowledge or information that any of the side-walks lying outside the line allowed for projections as aforesaid are in any manner obstructed or incumbered, to require the occupant or owner of the premises in front of which such obstruction or encumbrance exists, to remove the same; and if such occupant or owner shall neglect for the space of twenty-four hours to comply with such requisition, the Marshal shall forthwith cause such obstruction or encumbrance to be removed: *Provided*, That the provisions of this ordinance shall not be construed to apply to posts for awnings which are now standing, nor to shade trees or the boxes to protect them, nor to obstructions necessarily occasioned by the erection or repairing of buildings; but in such case no person shall obstruct more than one-half of the street and one-half of the side-walk opposite the premises occupied by such person, without leave first obtained from the Common Council.

Sec. 6. Excepting for the purpose of ingress and egress to and from yards across the side-walks, no person shall drive, ride, or lead, or suffer to remain, any horse, cart, carriage or team of any kind, on any of the side-walks within the City; nor shall he leave any horse, team or vehicle standing on any of the cross-walks in said City.

Sec. 7. Any person who shall wilfully offend against any of the provisions of this ordinance shall forfeit and pay a fine not exceeding twenty-five dollars.

Made and passed in Common Council this 17th day of June, A. D. 1851.

GEO. SEDGWICK, Mayor.

HENRY W. WELLES, Recorder.

No. 8.

AN ORDINANCE RELATIVE TO THE PUNISHMENT OF IDLE AND DISORDERLY PERSONS.

Be it Ordained by the Mayor, Recorder and Aldermen of the City of Ann Arbor—

SECTION 1. That any person or persons who may commit a breach or disturbance of the public peace, or shall by noise or otherwise, disturb any meeting within said City of Ann Arbor, shall, on conviction thereof before any Justice of the Peace in said City, be punished by a fine not exceeding twenty dollars and costs of prosecution, and may be imprisoned not exceeding ten days, or both, at the discretion of said Justice.

* Sec. 2. Any vagrant, lewd, idle or disorderly person, or any person intoxicated or drunk with liquors of any kind, common night-walkers, pilferers, or any person wanton, lascivious, obscene or vulgar of speech, conduct or behavior, common railers or brawlers, shall, upon conviction before any Justice of the Peace, be punished by fine not exceeding twenty-five dollars and costs of suit, or be imprisoned not exceeding thirty days, or both, at the discretion of the Justice.

Sec. 3. It shall be the duty of the Marshal to arrest all persons who may be found intoxicated within this City, and all persons offending under this act, and, without unreasonable delay, bring him, her or them before a Justice of the Peace in said City for trial, and if in the opinion of said Justice, any person brought before him is unfit, by reason of intoxication, to be tried immediately, it shall be his duty to order such person to be committed to the county jail for such time as he may judge necessary, not exceeding forty-eight hours, previous to trial.

Made and passed in Common Council in the City of Ann Arbor, this 24th day of June, 1851.

GEO. SEDGWICK, Mayor.

HENRY W. WELLES, Recorder.

No. 9.

AN ORDINANCE TO PROVIDE FOR THE APPOINTMENT OF FENCE VIEWERS.

Be it Ordained by the Mayor, Recorder and Aldermen of the City of Ann Arbor—

That it shall and may be lawful for the Common Council, annu-

---

*This section embraces the amendments made by Ordinance No. "9, which is omitted in its order.

ally, to appoint one Fence Viewer in each ward, who shall hold their offices until the first Monday in June next after their appointment, and until their successors shall be appointed and qualified, who shall, before entering upon the duties of their office, take the usual oath of office, and who shall severally have the same powers and be authorized to perform the same duties, and be entitled to the same compensation, and liable to the same penalties for neglect of duty, as Fence Viewers under Chapter 18, Title IV. of the Revised Statutes of the State of Michigan, passed and approved May 18, 1846.

Made and passed in Common Council at the City of Ann Arbor this 4th day of August, 1851.

GEO. SEDGWICK, Mayor.

HENRY W. WELLES, Recorder.

No. 10.

AN ORDINANCE DECLARING THE RECORDER OF THE CITY EX-OFFICIO CITY CLERK.

Be it Ordained by the Mayor, Recorder and Aldermen of the City of Ann Arbor—

That the Recorder of the City of Ann Arbor be, and he is hereby declared to be, ex-officio City Clerk of the City of Ann Arbor.

Made and passed in Common Council, this 30th day of September, 1851.

W. C. VOORHEIS, President pro tem.

HENRY W. WELLES, Recorder.

No. 11.

AN ORDINANCE RELATIVE TO CITY WARDS.

Be it Ordained by the Mayor, Recorder and Aldermen of the City of Ann Arbor—

That an alteration be made in the boundaries of the First and Second Wards of said City, as follows: The First shall embrace all that portion of the City lying east of Fourth street and south of Huron street; The Second Ward shall embrace all that portion of the City lying south of Huron street and west of Fourth street. Said division is made by the actual or supposed continuation of the center line of each of said streets in the present direction thereof to the limits of the City.

Made and passed in Common Council this 22d day of March, A. D. 1852.

GEO. SEDGWICK, Mayor.

HENRY W. WELLES, Recorder.

No. 12.

AN ORDINANCE RELATIVE TO THE ASSESSMENT AND COLLECTION OF A POLL TAX, AND TO STREETS.

Be it Ordained by the Mayor, Recorder and Aldermen of the City of Ann Arbor—

SECTION 1. That it shall be the duty of the Street Commissioner each year, between the first Monday of April and the first day of July, to make out a list of all white male inhabitants of said City over the age of twenty-one years, and under the age of fifty years, and make return of the same to the Common Council, who shall assess each one except paupers, lunatics, idiots, and members of fire companies in the City.

Sec. 2. When such return and assessment is made, the Mayor and Recorder shall issue a warrant to the Street Commissioner, directing him to collect said tax and make return of the same within three months from the date of the warrant.

Sec. 3. The Street Commissioner shall call on each one named in such warrant, and demand the money, and in case the person so assessed elects to pay a day's labor, the Commissioner shall give notice of the time and place when and where such labor is required.

Sec. 4. If the person shall refuse or neglect to perform said labor at the time and place required, or pay to the Commissioner the said sum of money, the Commissioner shall levy upon any property belonging to such person, and advertise and sell so much thereof as is necessary to pay the sum assessed, together with such fees as constables are by law allowed for such services.

* Sec. 5. In all cases where any portion of a public street, sidewalk, lane or alley shall be enclosed or obstructed by a fence or other obstruction, the Commissioner shall give notice to the owner or occupant of the premises along which is such fence or obstruction to cause the same to be removed forthwith, and in case of refusal or neglect of the owner or occupant to remove the same within five days of the time of such notice, the Street Commissioner shall remove or cause the same to be removed, and the owner or occupant of the land enclosed by said fence shall be liable to a fine of five dol-

---

* Sections five and six embrace the amendments made by Ordinance No. 16, which is omitted in its order.

lars, and a further fine of five dollars for every day after the five days such obstruction shall remain.

Sec. 6. Any person who shall hereafter build or put up, or cause the same to be done, any fence, building or other obstruction, encroaching upon any side-walk, street, lane or alley within the bounds of the City, shall be liable to a fine of five dollars, and all costs of removing the same, and the Street Commissioner shall cause the same to be removed.

Made and passed in Common Council this 24th day of May, A. D., 1852.

GEO. SEDGWICK, Mayor.

HENRY W. WELLES, Recorder.

No. 13.

AN ORDINANCE RELATIVE TO MAD DOGS.

Be it Ordained by the Mayor, Recorder and Aldermen of the City of Ann Arbor—

SECTION 1. That whenever the Mayor or Recorder and any Alderman shall deem it necessary, to protect the inhabitants of the City from Mad Dogs, they may direct the Marshal to kill every dog which shall be found running at large within the City, without being securely muzzled so as effectually to prevent such dog from biting any person.

Sec. 2. Be it further Ordained, That the Marshal, whenever so directed by the officers mentioned in section 1 of this ordinance, shall kill any vicious or ferocious dog found running at large in the City.

This Ordinance shall be in force from and after its passage.

Made and passed in Common Council this 16th day of August, A. D., 1852.

GEO. SEDGWICK, Mayor.

HENRY W. WELLES, Recorder.

No. 14.

AN ORDINANCE RELATIVE TO CATTLE RUNNING AT LARGE.

Be it Ordained by the Mayor, Recorder and Aldermen of the City of Ann Arbor—

SECTION 1. That it shall not be lawful for any horses or cattle of any kind to go at large within the City of Ann Arbor, at any time between the middle of November and the middle of March, nor at any time between nine o'clock in the evening and daylight the next morning, between the middle of March and the middle of November in each year; and if any horse, mare, cow, bull, ox, heifer or steer shall be found going at large within the limits of said City during any of the times above mentioned, it shall be lawful for any person, and it shall be the duty of the Marshal of the City, to drive the same to pound, for which the Marshal, or any person employed by him for that purpose, shall be entitled to receive the sum of ten cents for each animal so driven to pound.

Sec. 2. It shall be lawful for the Marshal to demand and receive as his fee for taking in and discharging each and every animal so impounded by virtue of this ordinance, ten cents; which fee, together with the fees for driving such animal to pound, and the reasonable charges for keeping and feeding the same therein, not exceeding twenty-five cents per day for each animal, shall be paid to the Marshal by the owner thereof, or some other person for him, before such animal shall be released from said pound: and if the owner of any such animal impounded as aforesaid, shall not pay the fee for impounding and the reasonable charges for keeping the same, within three days after the same were impounded, then it shall be the duty of the Marshal to sell such animal at public vendue, giving three days previous notice thereof, by advertisements posted up at such pound and the nearest public house thereto, and from the moneys accruing from such sale, to retain the fees for impounding and keeping such animal, together with ten per cent upon the avails of such sale for advertising and selling such animal, and to return the surplus to the owner of such animal; and if no owner shall appear and demand the same within six months after such sale, the same shall be paid into the City treasury, subject to the order of the Common Council.

Sec. 3. It shall be the duty of the Marshal to carry the provisions of this ordinance into effect; and upon complaint and conviction before any Justice of the Peace in said City, of a refusal or neglect, after due notice, to drive to pound any horse, mare, cow, bull, ox, heifer or steer found going at large as aforesaid, or to impound any such animal driven to pound by any other person according to the provisions of this ordinance, he shall be sentenced to pay a fine of one dollar for each neglect, together with costs of prosecution.

Sec. 4. This ordinance shall take effect and be in force from and after the 10th day of December next.

Made and passed in Common Council this 29th day of November, A. D. 1852.

GEO. SEDGWICK, Mayor.

HENRY W. WELLES, Recorder.

No. 15.

AN ORDINANCE RELATIVE TO IMPROVING SIDEWALKS.

Be it Ordained by the Mayor, Recorder and Aldermen of the City of Ann Arbor—

SECTION 1. That whenever, upon application in writing, of two-thirds of all the owners or occupants of real estate, subject to pay the tax for improving such sidewalks, the Common Council shall deem it proper to order the grading and planking, or making of any sidewalks in said City, such sidewalks shall be graded and planked, or constructed and made in such a manner, and of such materials, and of such width, as the Council shall upon such application direct, and under the superintendence of the Street Commissioner and such other officer as the Common Council shall appoint and direct, and under the direction of the Common Council; and the expenses of grading. planking or making such sidewalks (excepting the crosswalks over the parts of streets between the sidewalks) shall be assessed against the owners or occupants of the lots or portions of lots or premises which are in front of or adjoining such sidewalk, and the crosswalks or parts of such sidewalks crossing that part of any street lying between the sidewalks thereof, shall be constructed under the direction of the Common Council, by general tax.

Sec. 2. When the Common Council shall have ordered any sidewalk to be graded and planked, or otherwise improved, the Street Commissioner and Supervisor, or such other officer as the Common Council may appoint, shall ascertain as near as may be the expense of making such grading and planking or making, and shall make out and present to the Common Council a written report or assessment roll, stating the names of the owners or occupants of the lots or premises in front of or adjacent to such sidewalk which may be directed to be graded and planked or otherwise improved, describing with reasonable certainty each lot or portion of a lot owned or occupied by one person or company of persons, and also the names of such owner or occupant, or several owners or occupants, if they can be ascertained, and shall therein designate who of said owners or occupants are residents of said City, and who are non-residen s of said City, and shall also state the number of rods or feet and inches in length to be planked or otherwise improved in front of or adjacent to the lot or premises owned or occupied by each person, and the sum of money which each person or set of persons shall be assessed at, and pay for such grading, planking or improvement in proportion to the whole length of such sidewalks in front of or adjacent to the lot or portion of a lot owned or occupied by each separate person or set of persons, including with and adding to the length of the front of a lot or portion of a lot situated upon the corner of any block or at the intersections of any streets, the width of the sidewalk adjoining such corner or lot, and intersecting the sidewalk to be graded and planked or improved, unless such intersecting sidewalk shall have been graded and planked.

Sec. 3. The Common Council shall examine such report or assessment roll, and make such alterations and amendments therein as they may deem necessary or proper; and upon the approval of such report or assessment roll by the Common Council, the Recorder shall make out a notice directed to the several persons in such report named and proposed to be assessed, notifying them that they are about to be assessed to defray the expenses of grading and planking and otherwise improving the sidewalk in front of or adjacent to certain premises owned or occupied by them in said City, and that a report and assessment roll made out in the premises, is on file in the office of the Recorder, for inspection; and further notifying them when and where the Common Council will meet and review such assessment roll, on the request of any person considering himself aggrieved—which notice shall also set forth with reasonable certainty the place where such sidewalk is to be made, and the kind of sidewalk to be made, and that the party is allowed thirty days within which to make such grading and sidewalk, under the superintendence of the Street Commissioner and such other officer (naming him) as the Common Council may have designated for that purpose, and that if the same shall within that time have been so constructed to the satisfaction of such superintendents, no expense of proceedings to collect the same against the persons so constructing shall be incurred by them—which notice shall be published at least once each week for two successive weeks in some public newspaper published in said City; and in addition to such publication the Marshal shall cause a copy of such notice to be served upon all the persons therein named who are residents of said City, and upon the agents residing in said City who are known, of all non-resident owners therein named, by delivering the same to them or leaving such copy at their several places of abode or business in said City; and the Marshal shall return, under his oath of office, or the affidavit of the person serving the same, the time and manner of serving such notice; and at the expiration of thirty days after such publication and service, the Street Commissioner, or other officer appointed to superintend the construction of such sidewalk, shall report to the Common Council what part, if any, of said sidewalk has been completed, and what part, if any, has not been constructed; and if, from such report, it shall appear that any part of such sidewalk has not been constructed by the parties notified, it shall be the duty of the Recorder to make out from such report and the assessment roll, a tax roll, including all the property described and assessed in such report and assessment roll, the owners or occupants of which have neglected or omitted to grade and plank or construct such sidewalk, and submit the same to the Common Council; and the Common Council shall cause to be graded and constructed the part or parts of such sidewalk remaining unfinished; and the Common Council shall cause a warrant to be attached to such tax roll, authorizing and commanding the Treasurer to collect from the several persons named in such tax roll the several sums of money set opposite their respective names in the same manner as is provided for the collection of state, county and township taxes, and with like charges—and such warrant shall require the Treasurer to make return to the Common Council of his doings therein, in thirty days, and shall be signed by the Mayor and Recorder, and may be renewed from time to time, if the Common Council shall deem necessary; and the Treasurer shall have the same power to levy and collect the said several sums of money by distress and sale of goods and chattels which township treasurers have under the laws to collect state, county and township taxes; and it shall be the duty of the Treasurer, upon receiving such tax roll, to proceed and collect the taxes therein mentioned with all reasonable diligence; and if any of said taxes shall remain unpaid, and the collector shall not be able to collect the same within the time limited by such warrant, or any renewal thereof, it shall be the duty of the Treasurer, and such Treasurer is hereby authorized to make out and publish, in some newspaper published in said City, at least once in each week for five successive weeks, notice that unless the said sums, with the costs and charges thereon, shall be paid and satisfied before such sale, the premises described in such notice, and each separate parcel thereof, will, at the court house in said City, on some day not less than five weeks nor more than seven weeks from the first publication of such notice, be sold or leased for the shortest term of years at which any person will offer to take the same in consideration of advancing the sum or sums which were so assessed or taxed upon said land by the Common Council, together with the interest and all the costs and charges thereon, including the cost of such notice and of all proceedings relating to such sale, and of making the return and record thereof. If at the time mentioned in said notice, the owner or occupant, or person or persons liable to pay such tax, shall have neglected or refused to pay any such tax, with the costs and charges thereon, the Treasurer shall add to the amount of the tax, interest and costs then made upon each separate parcel of land, the sum of one dollar for the expenses of making such sale, and the return and record thereof, and of making the certificate to the purchasers upon such sale; and the Treasurer shall, at the time and place mentioned in said notice, commence the sale of such lands and continue the same from day to day (Sundays excepted) until the same shall be sold for a term of years for the purpose and in the manner above mentioned—but each lot or parcel of a lot owned by any one person, or set of persons and assessed separately, shall be sold by itself—and if any person or persons bidding at such sale shall fail to pay the amount of his or their respective bids on request, or agreeably to any notice given by the Treasurer on such sale, it shall be the duty of the Treasurer forthwith to re-sell the lands so remaining unpaid for—and no person having failed to pay his previous bids on request, shall be entitled to have his bids received at such sale. The Treasurer shall at the close of the sale, report to the Common Council the terms upon which each lot or parcel of land was sold, the amount bid therefor, the name and residence of the purchaser, and the length of the term for which each lot or parcel was sold—

and the Recorder shall make and keep a record of such sale, and any person claiming any interest in the premises as sold, may redeem any lot or parcel of land sold separately, within one year from the time of such sale, by paying the amount for which the same was sold, with interest at the rate of fifteen per cent per annum to the Treasurer, and taking duplicate receipts therefor, and delivering the same to the Recorder, who shall retain one, and enter the redemption of the lands therein described upon the record of such sale, and shall conntersign the other and deliver the same to the person so redeeming. Upon such sale the Treasurer shall give to the purchasers, upon the payment of their bids, a certificate in writing, duly numbered, describing the lands purchased, the amount paid therefor, and the length of time for which the land was sold, and the time when the purchaser will be entitled to a lease of the premises, unless sooner redeemed; and when any land so sold shall be redeemed, the Treasurer, upon the presentation of such certificate of purchase, sh.ll pay to the purchaser or his executors, administrators or assigns, the amount received by him upon the redemption of such lands, and take the proper receipt therefor; and if any lands so sold shall not have been redeemed within the time above provided for the redemption thereof, and it shall not appear that such land was improperly sold, on the presentation of such certificate of purchase to the Recorder, he shall prepare and deliver to such purchaser, his heirs or assigns, upon the payment by the lessee of the expense of such lease, not exceeding fifty cents, a lease of the premises so sold (in such form as the Common Council may prescribe) giving the purchaser or his heirs or assigns the use of the property so purchased by him for the time for which the same was sold, computing from the expiration of the time for redemption above provided; which lease shall be under seal, and signed by the Mayor and countersigned by the Recorder, and shall entitle the lessee and his heirs and assigns to the use of the land therein described, during the time therein mentioned, subject to all taxes legally assessed or to be assessed on such land.

Made and passed in Common Council this 22d day of March, A. D., 1853.

GEO. SEDGWICK, Mayor.

HENRY W. WELLES, Recorder.

No. 17.

AN ORDINANCE RELATIVE TO THE SALE OF FIRE WOOD.

Be it Ordained by the Mayor, Recorder and Aldermen of the City of Ann Arbor—

SECTION 1. The Common Council shall appoint one or more In-

6

spectors of Fire Wood, each of whom shall within ten days after such appointment, make and file with the Recorder an oath or affirmation to support the Constitution of the United States and the Constitution of the State of Michigan, and that they will honestly and faithfully discharge the duties of their office according to the best of their ability; and they shall also, before entering upon the duties of their office, give bonds to the Mayor, Recorder and Aldermen of the City of Ann Arbor, in such sum and with such sureties as the Common Council shall direct or approve, conditioned that they will honestly and faithfully discharge and perform all the duties which the ordinances or resolutions of the Common Council may from time to time require of them.

Sec. 2. It shall be the duty of each Inspector of Fire Wood, when required by either the seller or the purchaser of any fire wood brought within the limits of the City of Ann Arbor for sale, to inspect and measure the same, and to give a certificate of the date and amount of such measurement in words at full length; and he shall receive for every load or cord of wood so inspected and measured, the sum of six cents, to be paid by the person requiring the same, and all wood so inspected and measured shall be computed to contain one hundred and twenty-eight cubic feet, well stowed and packed, to the cord, and allowance being made for uneven and crooked sticks, and for being loosely packed.

Sec. 3. It shall be the duty of every person bringing cord or fire wood into said City for sale by the cord, in wagons, sleighs or other vehicles, to take the same to that part of the north side of Huron street, or the east side of Main street, adjoining the Court House Square, to be inspected and measured as aforesaid, and every person who shall suffer or permit his wagon, sleigh or other vehicle, loaded with wood for sale, to stand or remain in any of the streets of said City, within forty rods of the Court House Square, other than at the place above specified, or who shall sell or offer to sell in said City, fire wood by the load, without first having the same inspected and measured, and obtaining a certificate thereof as aforesaid, shall forfeit for the first offence the sum of one dollar and costs of prosecution, and for every subsequent offence the sum of five dollars and costs of prosecution.

Sec. 4. If any person within the limits of said City having obtained such certificate shall sell or dispose of such wood contrary to said certificate, or shall attempt to impose a false certificate in the sale thereof, or shall in any manner violate the provisions of this ordinance, he shall for every such offence forfeit and pay a fine of five dollars and costs of prosecution.

Sec. 5. This ordinance shall be in force from and after the 20th day of November, 1853.

Made and passed in Common Council this 24th day of October, 1853.

E. M. GREGORY, President pro tem.

C. N. FOX, Recorder.

No. 18.

AN ORDINANCE RELATIVE TO PUBLIC HEALTH.

Be it Ordained by the Mayor, Recorder and Aldermen of the City of Ann Arbor—

SECTION 1. That from and after the passage of this ordinance, and actual notice or due publication thereof, it shall be the duty of each and every physician of this City or other person practising as such, upon being called to visit any patient who shall prove to be sick of small pox, varioloid or cholera, to give immediate notice of the same, together with the name and residence of such patient, to the Mayor, Recorder, or any Alderman of said City, to the end that the Board of Health of said City may take such action in relation thereto as may be necessary for the preservation of the public health.

Sec. 2. Any physician or other person practising as such who shall fail to give notice as provided in the preceding section, shall upon conviction thereof be subject to a fine of not less than ten nor more than fifty dollars, with costs of prosecution.

Made and passed in Common Council this 6th day of January, A. D., 1855.

PHILIP BACH, President pro tem.

C. N. FOX, Recorder.

No. 19.

AN ORDINANCE RELATIVE TO HORSES AND CATTLE RUNNING AT LARGE.

Be it Ordained by the Mayor, Recorder and Aldermen of the City of Ann Arbor—

SECTION 1. That it shall not be lawful for any horse, mare, mule, bull, ox, steer or sheep to go at large within the City of Ann Arbor at any time between the middle of March and the middle of November of each year, and if any horse, mare, mule, bull, ox, steer or sheep shall be found going at large within the limits of said City within the time above mentioned, it shall be lawful for any person, and it shall be the duty of the Marshal of the City, to drive the same to pound, for which the Marshal or any person employed by him for that purpose, shall be entitled to receive the sum of ten cents for each animal so driven to pound, and the Marshal shall be entitled to the same fees, and shall proceed in the same manner in relation to said animals after being impounded, as is provided for in the "Ordinance [No. 14] relative to Cattle running at large," passed by the Common Council the 29th day of November, A. D. 1852.

Made and passed in Common Council this 28th day of May, A. D. 1855.

JAMES KINGSLEY, Mayor.

N. B. NYE, Recorder.

No. 20.

AN ORDINANCE FOR THE PROTECTION OF FRUIT, SHADE AND ORNAMENTAL TREES.

Be it Ordained by the Mayor, Recorder and Aldermen of the City of Ann Arbor—

SECTION 1. Any person owning or occupying land adjoining any street not less than four rods wide, may plant or set out trees on the side of said street contiguous to his land, which shall be set out in regular rows, at a distance of at least six feet from each other, and within ten feet of the margin of said street. And if any person shall cut down, destroy or injure any tree that may have been, or shall be, so planted or set out, or which shall have been left on the side of said street for shade, he shall be liable in treble damages to the owner or occupant of such adjoining land, in an action of trespass, or on the case.

Sec. 2. Every person who shall wilfully and maliciously or wantonly, and without cause, cut down or destroy, or otherwise injure any fruit tree, or any other tree, not his own, standing or growing for shade, ornament, or other useful purposes, or shall maliciously or wantonly break down, injure, mar or deface any fence belonging to or enclosing any lands not his own, or throw down or open any gate, bars or fence and leave the same down or open, shall be punished by imprisonment in the county jail not more than thirty days, or by fine not exceeding one hundred dollars.

Sec. 3. It shall not be lawful for any person to hitch any horse, mare, mule or other animal to any fruit, shade or ornamental tree within the City of Ann Arbor, and any person hitching or tying any of the animals aforesaid to any such fruit, shade or ornamental tree, shall be liable to the owner or occupant of the land in front or upon which said tree is situated, in treble damages for any damage any such animals may do to any said tree, in an action of trespass or on the case.

Sec. 4. The owner of any horse, mare, mule, cow, bull, ox, heifer, steer, sheep, swine or other animals running at large within the City of Ann Arbor at any time, shall be liable in treble damages for any damage any of said animals may do to any fruit, shade or ornamental tree, shrub or vine, whether the same be enclosed within any city lot, or set out, or left standing in front thereof, to the owner or occupant thereof, in an action of trespass or on the case.

Made and passed in Common Council at the City of Ann Arbor this 28th day of May, 1855.

JAMES KINGSLEY, Mayor.

N. B. NYE, Recorder.

No. 21.

AN ORDINANCE TO PREVENT OBSTRUCTING STREETS.

Be it Ordained by the Mayor, Recorder and Aldermen of the City of Ann Arbor—

That it shall not be lawful for any person to leave any horse, cart, wagon, carriage, sleigh, or other vehicle whatever, standing in any street within said City of Ann Arbor, so as to obstruct the free passage of said streets. Nor shall any person run or race any horse, or drive any horse or horses, or any carriage or vehicle at a faster rate than six miles per hour in any of the streets of said City; and any person offending against any of the provisions of this ordinance, shall upon conviction thereof be fined not exceeding fifty dollars for each offence, or be imprisoned in the county jail not exceeding thirty days.

Made and passed in Common Council, this 4th day of June, 1855.

JAMES KINGSLEY, Mayor.

N. B. NYE, Recorder.

No. 23.

AN ORDINANCE RELATIVE TO THE EXPOSURE OF PERSONS BY BATHING OR OTHERWISE.

Be it Ordained by the Mayor, Recorder and Aldermen of the City of Ann Arbor—

That it shall not be lawful for any person or persons to expose their naked bodies by bathing or otherwise within the limits of said City of Ann Arbor between sunrise in the morning and eight o'clock in the evening; and any person or persons offending against this ordinance shall upon conviction thereof be fined not exceeding twenty-five dollars, or imprisonment in the county jail not exceeding thirty days.

Made and passed in Common Council in the City of Ann Arbor, this 18th day of June, 1855.

JAMES KINGSLEY, Mayor.

N. B. NYE, Recorder.

No. 24.

AN ORDINANCE RELATIVE TO PAYING OVER MONEYS RECEIVED FOR FINES.

Be it Ordained by the Mayor, Recorder and Aldermen of the City of Ann Arbor—

That whenever any fine or penalty, under any of the ordinances of the City of Ann Arbor, shall be imposed upon any person or persons, and the same shall be paid to any Justice of the Peace, Marshal, Sheriff, Constable or other person, the said Justice of the Peace, Marshal, Sheriff, Constable, or other person receiving said penalty or fine, shall immediately pay the same over to the Treasurer of said City of Ann Arbor, taking from said Treasurer duplicate receipts therefor, and filing one of said receipts in the office of the Recorder of said City; and any person who shall neglect or refuse to pay over any such money so received, for the space of ten days after receiving the same, shall upon conviction thereof be fined not exceeding one hundred dollars, or imprisoned in the county jail not exceeding thirty days, or both, in the discretion of the Court.

Made and passed by the Common Council, this 18th day of June, 1855.

JAMES KINGSLEY, Mayor.

N. B. NYE, Recorder.

No. 25.

AN ORDINANCE RELATIVE TO BREACHES OF THE PEACE AND DISORDERLY CONDUCT.

Be it Ordained by the Mayor, Recorder and Aldermen of the City of Ann Arbor—

SECTION 1. Any person who may hereafter be found lurking,

lying in wait, or concealed in any house or other building, or any yard or premises within the limits of the City of Ann Arbor, with intent to do any mischief, or to pilfer, or commit any crime or misdemeanor whatever, shall, for every such offence, on conviction thereof, be punished by a fine not exceeding one hundred dollars, or imprisonment in the county jail not exceeding thirty days, or both, at the discretion of the Court, and may moreover be held to bail for good behavior.

Sec. 2. Any person who shall make, aid, countenance or assist in making, any noise, riot, disturbance, cheverie, by blowing horns, ringing bells or other improper diversion or noise, or who shall be guilty of any indecent, immoral or insulting conduct, language or behavior in the streets or elsewhere in said City, and all persons who shall collect in bodies or crowds in said City for unlawful purposes, to the annoyance or disturbance of the citizens or travelers, or so as to impede the free passage of any street or sidewalk in said City, shall for each offence, on conviction thereof, be liable to the punishment mentioned in the foregoing section.

Sec. 3. Any person or persons who shall, within the limits of said City, keep a disorderly or ill-governed house or place, or a house or place for the resort of persons of evil name or fame, or of dishonest conversation, or who shall procure, or suffer to come together at such house or place, persons of evil name or fame, or who shall commit or suffer to be committed therein, any immoral, indecent, or improper conduct or behavior; or any tippling, reveling, prostitution, rioting or disturbance, every person or persons so offending, or who shall aid or assist in any manner, in offending in the premises, shall on conviction thereof, be liable to the punishment mentioned in the first section of this ordinance.

Sec. 4. No person shall raise or fly any kite in any of the streets, lanes or alleys; or within the limits of the City of Ann Arbor, under a penalty for each offence not exceeding twenty dollars, or confinement in the county jail not exceeding ten days, and costs of prosecution.

Sec. 5. No person or persons shall, unless especially authorized by the Common Council, dig, remove or carry away any earth, loam, sand, gravel or sod, from any of the streets, lanes or alleys, or public grounds within the limits of the said City, under a penalty for each offence not exceeding fifty dollars and costs of prosecution.

Sec. 6. It shall not be lawful for any person to leave any cart, wagon, carriage or sleigh, wood, timber or any other incumbrance or obstruction in any of the streets, lanes or alleys of said City during the night season; and any person offending herein, on conviction, shall pay a fine not exceeding twenty dollars and costs of prosecution, and it shall be the duty of the Marshal to remove all such obstructions.

Sec. 7. It shall not be lawful for any person or persons, unless authorized by the Common Council in writing, to occupy any portion or part of the public streets or sidewalks with any tent, shanty, shop, table or building for the retail sale of any liquors, groceries, cakes, pies or merchandise; and every person offending against the provisions of this section shall on conviction be fined a sum not exceeding ten dollars and costs of prosecution, and it shall be the duty of the Marshal to remove such tent, shanty, shop, table or building, as a public nuisance.

Sec. 8. No person shall leave any horse or horses attached to any cart, wagon, carriage or other vehicle in any part of the public streets of said City without being sufficiently tied or hitched, under a penalty not exceeding ten dollars and costs of prosecution, for each offence.

Sec. 9. For any breach of any of the ordinances of said City of Ann Arbor, in the night time, it shall be the duty of the Marshal, Sheriff, or any Constable, to arrest the persons, and either take them forthwith before a magistrate, or commit them for safe keeping in any safe place in said City, until nine o'clock the next day, unless that shall be Sunday, in which case he shall be committed until Monday, and then bring him before a magistrate for examination.

Made and passed in Common Council, in the City of Ann Arbor, this 4th day of August, A. D. 1856.

W. S. MAYNARD, Mayor.

N. B. NYE, Recorder.

No. 27.

AN ORDINANCE RELATIVE TO GONGS.

Be it Ordained by the Mayor, Recorder and Aldermen of the City of Ann Arbor—

That it shall not be lawful for any person to ring or sound any Gong upon any of the streets, lanes, alleys, or sidewalks, or outside of any building fronting thereon, within said City; and any person offending against the provisions of this ordinance, shall upon conviction thereof be fined a sum not less than one dollar, nor more than five dollars, and costs of prosecution, for each offence.

Made and passed in Common Council, in the City of Ann Arbor, this 10th day of November, 1856.

W. S. MAYNARD, Mayor.

N. B. NYE, Recorder.

No. 28.

AN ORDINANCE RELATIVE TO DISORDERLY CONDUCT.

Be it Ordained by the Mayor, Recorder and Aldermen of the City of Ann Arbor—

SECTION 1. If any person shall, on the arrival or departure of any railroad cars at or from said City, or for the period of thirty minutes after the arrival or before the departure of said cars, and within twenty rods of the place where said cars have or are about to stop or depart from said City, make, aid, countenance or assist in making any loud or boisterous noise, disturbance or improper diversion, or shall be guilty of any indecent, immoral, obscene or insulting conduct, language or behavior, such person shall, for every such offence, upon conviction thereof, be fined in a sum not exceeding one hundred dollars and costs of prosecution, or be confined in the county jail not exceeding sixty days.

Sec. 2. If any person shall, during the night time, remove any boxes, barrels, wood, lumber, stones or any other thing not his own, from any of the sidewalks, yards or buildings, into any of the streets, lanes or alleys of said City, or upon the premises of any other person, such person shall, upon conviction thereof, be fined in a sum not exceeding one hundred dollars and costs of prosecution, or be confined in the county jail not exceeding sixty days.

Sec. 3. In all cases where prosecutions are commenced under any of the ordinances of said City, the magistrate before whom the same shall be tried, may in his discretion add to the penalty attached thereto, the costs of prosecution.

Made and passed in Common Council in the City of Ann Arbor, this 18th day of February, 1857.

W. S. MAYNARD, Mayor.

N. B. NYE, Recorder.

No. 29.

AN ORDINANCE RELATIVE TO HACKS, CABS, DRAYS AND OTHER VEHICLES.

Be it Ordained by the Mayor, Recorder and Aldermen of the City of Ann Arbor—

SECTION 1. The Common Council may license any trustworthy person, of the age of twenty-one years, to keep Hacks, Cabs, Drays or other vehicles, for hire, upon such applicants complying with this chapter, in giving proper security, and upon paying two dollars and fifty cents for every Hack, Cab, Dray or other vehicle of which the owner thereof resides within this City, and five dollars and fifty cents where the owner thereof resides out of this City; and such license shall state the number of each Hack, Cab, Dray or other vehicle, with the name of the person to whom it is granted; and it shall in all cases continue in force until the first day of May next ensuing the date thereof; and no person shall keep or use any Hack, Cab, Dray or other vehicle for hire in said City without being licensed as aforesaid, under the penalty of ten dollars and costs of prosecution for each offence.

Sec. 2. Every person to whom such a license shall be granted, shall execute a bond with one or more sufficient securities, to be approved by the Common Council, in the penalty of fifty dollars, conditional that he will pay all penalties and damages for which he may become liable on account of such Hacks, Cabs, Drays or other vehicles.

Sec. 3. The price that may be charged by the owners or drivers of Hacks, Cabs, or other vehicles, shall not be exceeding as follows, viz: For conveying a single person, for each drive less than an hour, twenty-five cents each; for conveying two or more persons, for each drive less than an hour, twelve and a-half cents each; for the use of a hack or cab by the hour, to carry not more than four persons inside, at the rate of fifty cents per hour; for conveying a single person and trunk from the railroad depot to any place within said City, or from any place within said City to said depot, twenty-five cents, and for each additional trunk, ten cents; children under twelve years, at half the above rates. The price which may be charged by the owner or driver of any dray shall not be exceeding twenty-five cents for one trunk, when but one is carried, and ten cents for each additional one. When a hack or cab is taken by the hour, the owner or driver thereof shall receive the price allotted to a full hour, whether the same be consumed or not, and after the first hour the charge shall be for the fractional parts of hours, rateably, and not full hours.

Sec. 4. The penalty of ten dollars and costs of prosecution shall be imposed upon the owner or driver of any Hack, Cab Dray or other vehicle, and recovered before any Justice of the Peace, who shall,

First, Unreasonably refuse or neglect to convey any person or persons to any place within the limits of the City, when applied to for that purpose, and being at the time unemployed;

Second, Or demand or receive any greater prices or rates than those herein established;

Third, Or neglect or refuse to place upon his Hack, Cab, Dray or other vehicle, in a conspicuous place, a card containing the license, the name of the owner, and the rates of fare, legibly printed or painted.

Sec. 5. No hotel keeper who may keep an Omnibus or Carriage for the purpose of conveying travelers to and from the railroad depot, shall be permitted to use the same for carrying any person or persons for hire in and through said City, except on taking out a

No. 32.

AN ORDINANCE RELATIVE TO HORSES AND CATTLE.

Be it Ordained by the Mayor, Recorder and Aldermen of the City of Ann Arbor—

SECTION 1. That it shall not be lawful for any person to ride, drive or lead any horse, cow or ox on or along any sidewalk within said City, or leave the same standing thereon; and any person offending against the provisions of this section shall, upon conviction thereof, be fined not less than one dollar, nor more than ten dollars, and costs of prosecution, for each offence.

Sec. 2. It shall not be lawful for any person to tie or hitch any horses or oxen for the purpose of feeding, in Main. Huron, Ann, Catherine, Washington, or Liberty streets, between First and State street, and any person offending against the provisions of this section shall be liable to the same penalty as in the preceding section.

Sec. 3. In any case where the second section of this ordinance, or section eight of ordinance No. 25 is violated or broken, it shall be the duty of the Marshal to take said horses or oxen to pound, and said Marshal shall charge and receive for so doing the same fees as are allowed by the ordinances of the City for impounding horses and cattle.

W. S. MAYNARD, Mayor.

N. B. NYE, Recorder.

No. 33.

AN ORDINANCE RELATIVE TO GAS WORKS.

WHEREAS. it is desirable that this City shall be lighted with Gas, and in order to induce any company to undertake to supply gas for that purpose it is necessary to secure to such company certain exclusive rights and privileges, subject to certain restrictions and conditions; and Whereas, the Ann Arbor Gas Light Company, a corporation recently formed in Ann Arbor for that purpose, has proposed to light the City with gas upon the terms hereinafter mentioned—Therefore,

Be it Ordained by the Mayor, Recorder and Aldermen of the City of Ann Arbor—

That the exclusive right and privilege of erecting Gas Works within this City, and of laying and continuing gas pipes along and across any and all of the streets, sidewalks, lanes, alleys and public grounds in said City, and of manufacturing gas in said City for sale for light, and of supplying said City and the buildings and streets therein with gas for lighting the same, be and is hereby granted and secured to the "Ann Arbor Gas Light Company," upon the conditions and under the restrictions hereinafter mentioned, so long as said company shall continue to supply gas for lighting said City, and shall comply with the restrictions and conditions hereinafter mentioned; *Provided however*, and this grant is made subject to the following restrictions and conditions, to wit: That said company shall within sixty days make and file with the Recorder, to be recorded and preserved, a copy of the articles of association of said company, and a written assent of said company to the provisions of this ordinance, and the agreement by the said company, signed by the officers of said company to erect gas works in said City, and to manufacture and supply gas as hereinafter mentioned; that said company shall within three months commence the erection of gas works in said City, and shall within one year lay down at least fifteen thousand feet of main gas pipe in said City, and shall supply and continue to supply all persons along the lines of such main pipe who may suitably supply their premises and buildings with service pipe and fixtures for receiving and burning gas, and who may require and pay for the same and sign the rules and regulations usual with gas companies, with gas of as good quality as that furnished by the Detroit gas company, at a rate not exceeding, exclusive of a reasonable rent for meters, four dollars per thousand cubic feet for private lights, and to the corporation of the City of Ann Arbor, for public lamps, at a rate not exceeding three dollars and fifty cents per thousand cubic feet; and that thereafter, as other parts of the City may become more compactly built, so as to afford responsible applicants as consumers of gas in twenty different buildings who shall agree to take and continue to use and pay for gas therein for each additional one thousand feet of main pipe, the said company shall within a reasonable time after such application for that purpose extend gas pipes and furnish gas upon the terms aforesaid to such additional buildings of said applicants; and that said company, in digging for and laying gas pipes, shall take care not unnecessarily or unreasonably to obstruct or injure any street, sidewalk, lane or alley, and shall with reasonable diligence restore such street, sidewalk, lane or alley to as good a state of repair as the same was in before disturbed by said company, and shall in all respects fully indemnify and save harmless the City of Ann Arbor from and against all damages or costs which the City may be put to or sustain by reason of such digging; and in case the dividends of said company shall average to exceed fifteen per cent per annum, the Common Council may, at any time, after giving to said company thirty days notice to show cause against such reduction, have power to compel the said company to make a reduction in the price of gas equivalent to the excess of its dividends over fifteen per cent per annum, the reduction to be pro rata to the citizens and the corporation; and it is further agreed that the said "Ann Arbor Gas Light Company" shall locate their gas works on block seven, eight, ten or eighteen of

Page & Ormsby's Addition, or at such other point as the Common Council and Board of Directors may agree upon.

Made and passed in Common Council this 2d day of April, A. D., 1858.

W. S. MAYNARD, Mayor.

N. B. NYE, Recorder.

———

No. 34.

AN ORDINANCE AMENDATORY OF ORDINANCE NO. 4, RELATIVE TO THE PREVENTION OF FIRES.

Be it Ordained by the Mayor, Recorder and Aldermen of the City of Ann Arbor—

That ordinance No. 4, being "An Ordinance Relative to the Prevention of Fires," be and the same is hereby amended by inserting in section eleven, fourth line, after the words court house square, " without permission of the Common Council."

Made and passed in Common Council this 7th day of March, A. D., 1859.

PHILIP BACH, Mayor.

ROBERT J. BARRY, Recorder.

AMENDMENTS TO CHARTER.

An Act to amend "an act to incorporate the City of Ann Arbor," approved April fourth, one thousand eight hundred and ~~fifty~~ one.

Section 1. The people of the State of Michigan enact, That section one of "An act to incorporate the City of Ann Arbor," approved April fourth, eighteen hundred and fifty-one, be amended so that the same shall read as follows:

Section 1. That so much of the township of Ann Arbor in the County of Washtenaw, as is included in the following limits (including the present City of Ann Arbor), to wit: The south three-fourths of section number twenty; The south three-fourths of the west three-fourths, of section number twenty-one; The west three-fourths of section number twenty-eight; Entire section number twenty-nine; The north half of section number thirty-two; and the west three-fourths of the north half of section number thirty-three, in township two south, of range six east; and also, so much of the east half of the southeast quarter of section number twenty-one, and of the east half of the north-east quarter of section number twenty-eight, as lies west of the easterly bank of Huron River, and north of the south line of the Territorial Road crossing said river, on or near the line between said sections, be and the same is hereby set off from said township and declared to be a city by the name of the City of Ann Arbor.

8

Section 2. Section three of said act shall be amended so that the same may read as follows :

Section 3. The said City shall be divided into five wards, as follows : The First Ward shall embrace all that portion of the City lying south of Huron street and east of Fourth street ; the Second Ward shall embrace all that portion of the City lying south of Huron street and west of Fourth street ; the Third Ward shall embrace all that portion of the City lying north of Huron street, and south of the River Huron, and west of Fourth street ; the Fourth Ward shall embrace all that portion of the City lying north of Huron street, and south of the River Huron, and east of Fourth street ; and the Fifth Ward shall embrace all that part of the City lying northeast of the River Huron. The aforesaid division is made by the actual or supposed continuation of the centre line of each of said streets in the present direction thereof, to the limits of the wards : Provided, That the Common Council may at any time, alter the bounds of said wards, or any them, and may at any time, with the assent of the Board of Supervisors of the County of Washtenaw, by a majority vote of all the Supervisors elect, create an additional Ward, and may create an additional assessment district, or an additional assessment and collection district, when there shall be six wards.

Section 3. Section Four of said act shall be amended so that the same may read as follows :

Section 4. There shall be the following officers in and for said City, to wit : one Mayor, one Recorder, one Marshal, one Street Commissioner, one Attorney, one Treasurer, two Supervisors—one to be elected in the First and Second Wards, and one to be elected in the Third, Fourth and Fifth Wards, who shall be assessors in their respective districts ; one Collector. or such number of Collectors not exceeding one in each collection district in said City as the Common Council may by proper ordinance prescribe ; one Constable, to be elected in each Ward —all of which officers shall hold their offices for one year, and until their successors are elected or appointed, and qualified ; and two Aldermen, to be elected in each ward, who shall respectively hold their offices for one and two years, and until their successors are elected and qualified; and four Justices of the Peace, who shall respectively hold their offices for four years; and when by an ordinance to that effect, the Common Council shall with the assent mentioned in section three, have increased the number of wards to six, and the number of assessment districts to three, there shall be three Supervisors—one in the first and second Wards, one in the third and fourth Wards, and one in the fifth and sixth Wards, who shall be assessors in their respective districts, and shall respectively hold their offices for one year, and until their successors are elected and qualified.

Section 4. Section number Five of said act shall be amended so that the same shall read as follows:

Section 5. The inhabitants of said City having the qualifications of electors under the Constitution of the State, shall on the first Monday of April, in each year, at such place in each Ward as the Common Council shall designate, proceed to elect by plurality of votes by ballot, from among the qualified electors of said City, one Mayor, one Recorder, one Justice of the Peace, one Marshal, one Street Commissioner and one Collector, (or such number of Collectors, not exceeding one for each assessment district in said City, as the Common Council by proper ordinance have prescribed); and the inhabitants of each ward in said City, having the like qualifications of electors, shall at the same time and place, in their respective wards, proceed to elect one Alderman, to hold his office for two years, and until his successor shall be elected and qualified; and one Constable, and there shall also, at the same time, be elected one Supervisor by the qualified electors of the first and second Wards; and one Supervisor by the qualified electors of the third fourth and fifth Wards; Provided, That in each Ward, in which there shall at the time of such election be no Alderman having another year to serve, there shall be two Aldermen elected who shall be divided into classes as prescribed in section six of this act, unless the electors shall by their ballots designate which is to hold office for one year only: And provided also, That when the Common Council shall, with the assent aforesaid, by an ordinance to that effect, have increased the number of Wards to six, and and the number of assessment districts to three, there shall be elected three Supervisors—one in the first and second Wards, one in the third and fourth Wards, and one in the fifth and sixth Wards; And provided also, That such Justices, Supervisors, Constables, shall each of them have the like power and be subject to the same duties and liabilities as such officers respectively in the several townships of this State, and that such Collector or Collectors and each of them shall have the like power and be subject to the same duties and liabilities in relation to collecting taxes as township Treasurers in the several townships in this State; And provided further, That all actions within the jurisdiction of Justices of the Peace may be commenced and prosecuted in said Justices' Courts, when the Plaintiff or Defendant, or one of the Plaintiffs or Defendants, resides in a township adjoining the township of Ann Arbor, or in the townships of York, Saline, Freedom, or Lima.

Section 5. Section thirty-six of said act shall be amended so that the same shall read as follows:

Section 36. Whenever the Common Council shall be authorized by a vote of the property tax-payers of said City to raise a tax for any specific purpose, and which cannot be included in the assessment roll and collected or returned for non-payment as provided in section thirty-five of this act, it shall be lawful for the Common Council to apportion such tax upon the property taxable for such purpose, according to the valuation contained in the then last assessment roll, and shall place the tax in a column opposite the valuation of the property, and when such roll is completed, the Recorder shall make and deliver a copy thereof to the Collector or Collectors of the proper district or districts, together with a warrant or warrants, signed by the Mayor and Recorder, commanding the Collector to collect from the several persons named in said roll, the several sums mentioned in the last column of such roll opposite their respective names, and to account for and pay over to the City Treasurer, within a time in said warrant to be specified, not less than thirty days, nor more than ninety days from the date thereof, all moneys collected or received by each collector upon or by virtue of such roll, after deducting the Collector's fees upon the amounts collected, and to deliver such roll and warrant to the Recorder;

and such warrant shall authorize the Collector, in case any person named in said roll shall neglect or refuse to pay his tax, to levy the same by distress and sale of the goods and chattels of such person, and it shall be the duty of such Collector to collect such taxes within the time specified in such warrant, or within such further time as the Common Council may by resolution direct, and to account for and pay over to the City Treasurer all moneys collected, or received by him, upon or by virtue of such roll, after deducting such collector's fees upon the amount collected by him, and to deliver such roll and warrant to the Recorder, and in case any person shall neglect or refuse to pay the tax imposed on him, the Collector may levy the same by distress and sale of the goods and chattels of such person in the same manner as township Treasurers, and if any of the taxes mentioned in said roll shall remain unpaid, and the collector shall be unable to collect the same from the person taxed, he shall make out and deliver to the City Treasurer a full and perfect description of the premises, and a copy from said roll of the taxes so unpaid, and shall add thereto an affidavit, sworn to before an officer authorized to administer oaths for general purposes, that the sums mentioned in such statement remain unpaid, and that he has not, upon diligent search and enquiry been able to discover any goods and chattels belonging to the person taxed whereupon he could levy the same.

Section 6. Section forty-three of said act shall be amended so as to read as follows:

Section 43. The township of Ann Arbor shall retain its present organization, subject to the alteration of boundaries herein made and provided, and the next annual township meeting for said township shall be held at the Washtenaw House, in that part of said township above set off and annexed to the City of Ann Arbor, at which election there may be chosen in addition to the usual township officers, so many Justices of the Peace as may be necessary to fill any vacancies in the office of Justice of the Peace in said township occasioned by the alteration of its boundaries; and future township meetings, or elections for said township, or meetings of the Township Board may be held within said City of Ann Arbor, with the like effect in every respect as if held in said township, and the township Libary and the township Clerk's office may be kept in said City.

Section 7. The following sections shall be added to said act, to wit:

Section 48. The ordinances now in force in the village of Ann Arbor shall remain in force in that part of said village above annexed to the City of Ann Arbor until repealed, altered, or amended by the Common Council; and all sums of money heretofore raised for local improvements, on either side of the river, shall be expended on the side of the river, on which the same was raised; and all the property, rights, credits and effects of every kind belonging to said village are hereby absolutely vested in the City of Ann Arbor, and shall be delivered to the Common Council of said City.

Section 49. In making assessments in said City, and in apportioning the taxes for city purposes, the Supervisors shall so discriminate as not to impose upon the rural portions those expenses which belong exclusively to the built portions of the City, for which purpose they may, in their discretion, distinguish in their assessments, what properties are within the agricultural or rural sections, not having the benefit of lighting, watering, watching, or other expenditures for purposes exclusively for the benefit of the built and densely populated parts of the City, and all lands within such agricultural or rural districts, exclusively used for woodland, pasture, meadow, or farming purposes, may and shall be assessed to the owner, or occupant at their cash value, and by some suitable general description, and not as separate City Lots, and for such purpose the Common Council in preparing the certified statement to the Supervisor of the amount of taxes to be raised for general purposes, or purposes other than school, public buildings or street, or highway purposes, shall distinguish between the expenses which are properly chargeable upon the whole City, including (for collecting fees) one per cent. of the amount of all taxes to be raised in the City, and those which are exclusively for the benefit of the more densely populated parts of the City, and shall apportion to each assessment district its equitable proportion of the taxes for each purpose, and shall in such statement distinguish the amount of each class of such local expenses, and the Supervisors in apportioning such local expenses shall charge upon the property within the district to be benefited by such local expenditure the amount of the taxes therefor.

Section 50. Each Supervisor shall, on or before the fifteenth day of November, deliver to the Collector of his district, the tax roll or tax list of such district, with the taxes for the year annexed to each valuation and carried out in the last column thereof, the School Library and School House taxes in one column, the Highway or Street taxes in another, the City taxes in another, the County taxes in another, and the State taxes in another column, and if other taxes are at any time required by law they shall be placed each in another column, and the warrant for their collection shall specify particularly the several amounts and purposes for which said taxes are to be paid into the City and County Treasurers respectively.

Section 51. To such tax roll or tax list the Supervisor shall annex a warrant under his hand, directed to the Collector of his district, commanding him to collect from the several persons named in said roll, the several sums mentioned in the last column of such roll opposite their respective names, and to pay over to the County Treasurer the amounts therein specified for State and County purposes, and to pay over the remainder of said taxes (after deducting one per cent. of the amount collected by him as his fees for collecting), to the Treasurer of said City, on or before the first day of February, then next, and such warrant shall authorize the Collector, in case any person named in such roll shall neglect or refuse to pay his tax, with the fees for collecting, to be added, to levy the same by distress and sale of the goods and chattels of such person.

Section 52. Each Collector shall, immediately after the receipt of the tax roll and before the first day of December, post up in the Post Office in said City, and in as many as ten of the most public places in his collection district, conspicuous handbills giving notice where the tax roll can be seen, and taxes paid, and a receipt obtained therefor, without expense, at any time between nine o'clock, A. M. and four o'clock, P. M., during the month of December,. (Sundays and Christmas day only excepted), and the tax roll shall be kept at the place or places mentioned in such handbills, from nine o'clock, A. M. until four o'clock, P. M., each day during the month of December, (Sundays and Christmas day excepted), so that any person or persons can pay the tax assessed against him or them, and obtain the Collector's receipt therefor, and on all taxes so paid prior to the first day of January, no fee or per centage, besides the amount of tax specified in such roll, shall be charged or payable.

Section 53. The Common Council may by ordinance prescribe what amount not exceeding three per cent. nor less than one per cent., the Collector or Collectors may add for his fees to each tax remaining unpaid, on the first day of January ,upon his tax roll; and it shall be lawful for each Collector to add to each tax remaining unpaid on his roll, on the first day of January, such percentage as the Common Council may have prescibed for the Collector's fees, and to collect such percentage with such tax, in the same manner as he is. authorized to collect the tax, and for the purposes of collecting such taxes, by the Collector, such additional percentage shall be deemed and taken to be a part of the tax.

Section 54 Each Collector in said City shall and may proceed to collect the taxes in his collection district, and to pay over money to the County Treasurer, and to return to the County Treasurer a statement of the taxes remaining unpaid and due, in the manner provided by law for Township Treasurers, and all provisions of the laws of this State relating to the collection of taxes by Township Treasurers, or to the paying over money by Township Treasurers to the County Treasurer, or to the returning by the Township Treasurer to the County Treasurer, of a statement of the taxes remaining unpaid and due, are hereby made applicable to the Collector or Collectors of said City.

Section 55. Each Collector shall, on or before the first day of February, account for and pay over to the City Treasurer the full amount of all the taxes contained in his tax roll, deducting the amount to be paid to the County Treasurer, and deducting the amount of one per cent. upon all taxes collected by such Collector for the Collector's fees for collecting or receiving the same.

Section 56. The Common Council shall have power to make, enact, modify, amend and repeal such ordinances, by-laws, and regulations as they may deem necessary, or expedient within said City, for prohibiting, restraining, or regulating sports, theatres, caravans of animals, and other performances, or exhibitions, except exhibitions of Agricultural or Educational Societies, for money or pay, bathing, or swimming in any public water or place, indecent exposure of the person, horse-racing, ringing bells, crying goods, or commodities for sale or at auction, any disorderly noise, or disturbance, and for prohibiting, restraining, or regulating, within such parts of the City as they may deem expedient, and prescribe the building, rebuilding, enlarging, repairing, or placing any wooden buildings, the buying, selling, carrying, keeping, storing, using, or firing gunpowder, fire-crackers, or fire-works, making bonfires, butcher's shops or stalls, candle, soap, glue, or starch manufactories, establishments for rendering tallow, lard, or oil, and all establishments where any nauseous, offensive, or unwholesome business may be carried on; blacksmiths, coopers, cabinet makers, carpenters and joiners' shops, and all buildings, business, and establishments of any kind usually classed as extra-hazardous in respect to fire; and for preventing, suppressing and punishing street begging, soliciting alms, mock auctions, and every kind of fraudulent game, device, or practice; the sale of unwholesome meat, poultry, fish, vegetables, or other articles of food or provisions; impure, spurious, or adulterated wine, spirituous liquors or beer, or knowingly keeping or offering the same for sale; for preventing auctions, peddling, pawn brokerage, or using for hire carts, cabs, drays, hacks, or any kind of carriage or vehicle; or opening or keeping any tavern, hotel, victualing house, saloon, or other house or place for furnishing meals, food, or drink, or billiard tables or ball alleys, without first obtaining from the Common Council license therefor; for licensing and regulating carts, drays, cabs, hacks, and all carriages or vehicles kept or used for hire, auctioneers, peddlers, pawnbrokers, auctions, peddling, pawnbrokerage, taverns, hotels, victualing houses, saloons, and other houses or places for fur-

nishing meals, food, or drink, and keepers of billiard tables
and ball alleys, but not for gaming ; for establishing and regulating markets, market-places, booths or stands, public reservoirs, wells and pumps, and preventing the waste of water,
and may provide for obtaining, holding, regulating and mana-
ging burial grounds, within or without the City ; for keeping
sidewalks clear from boxes, dirt, snow, wood, or other obstructions, appointing watchmen and their duties and compensation ; the purity of the waters in the streams or ponds in the
City ; and for taking a census of the inhabitants of the City,
when deemed expedient, and regulating the same.

Section 57. Whenever in any Ward or Wards in said
City there shall not be two Aldermen to constitute the Board
of Registration of such Ward previous to any election, the
Common Council shall, in time, appoint suitable freeholders,
resident in such Wards, temporary Aldermen of such Wards,
who shall take the oath of office and have all the power of
Aldermen of such Ward, and shall hold their offices until the
close of the election, and of the canvass of the votes in such
Ward at the next election after such appointment, and shall,
during their continuance in office, act as and be members of
the Board of Registration of such Ward, and have all the
powers and perform all the duties of members of the Board
of Registration in such Ward.

Section 58. This act shall take effect immediately.

Approved February 25th, 1861.

ORDINANCES.

No. 35.

Be it ordained by the Mayor, Recorder, and Aldermen of the City of Ann Arbor:

That the time provided by ordinance No. 12, for the return to to the Common Council of the list of white male inhabitants of said City, is hereby extended to the first Monday of August, such extension to apply only to the present year.

Made and passed in Common Council, this 7th day of July, 1859. ROBERT J. BARRY, Mayor.

E. B. POND, Recorder, *pro tem.*

No. 36.

AN ORDINANCE RELATIVE TO STAGNANT WATER.

Be it ordained by the Mayor, Recorder and Aldermen of the City of Ann Arbor:

That if any person or persons owner of or occupying any lot or land within the boundaries of the City shall by filling up, taking up, injuring or in any manner obstructing any ditch, drain or acqueduct running through or over such lot or land, cause the water to flow back or become stagnant upon his, her or their premises, or the premises of any other person in said City, and thereby to become offensive, hurtful or unhealthy to the neighborhood or to travelers, it shall be the duty of the Marshal to give notice to the person or persons so offending, to open or restore such drain, ditch, or acqueduct, so as to draw off such stagnant water forthwith, and if such owner or occupant shall refuse or neglect for the space of twenty-four hours after such notice shall be given, to open and restore the same, he, she, or they, on conviction thereof, shall be liable to a fine of FIVE DOLLARS for every day such neglect or refusal shall continue. And whenever any nuisance is found to exist by reason of stagnant water which has become offensive, hurtful or unhealthy, on any lot or land in this City, and it shall be found that the same has been prevented from running off by the filling up, taking up, injuring or obstructing any ditch, drain, or aqueduct on any neighboring or adjoining lot or land by which the same was formerly drained, the person who filled up, took up, injured or obstructed such ditch, drain or aqueduct, shall be deemed guilty of creating such nuisance, and shall be liable on conviction, to a fine of FIVE DOLLARS for each day that such nuisance shall be permitted to remain after notice to him by the Marshal to remove the same.

Made and passed in Common Council, this 5th day of September, A. D. 1859.

E. B. POND, President, *pro tem.*

N. E. WELCH, Recorder.

No. 37.

AN ORDINANCE AMENDATORY OF ORDINANCE NO. 19, RELATIVE TO HORSES AND SWINE RUNNING AT LARGE.

Be it ordained by the Mayor, Recorder and Aldermen of the City of Ann Arbor:

That Ordinance number 19, "relative to horses and cattle running at large," be and the same is hereby amended by inserting after the word "sheep" in the second line of section one, the words "goose or duck," and also by inserting after the word "sheep" in the fifth line of said section one the words "goose or duck."

Made and passed in Common Council this 5th day of September, A. D. 1859,

E. B. POND, President, *pro tem.*

N. E. WELCH, Recorder.

No. 38.

AN ORDINANCE AMENDATORY OF ORDINANCE NO. 15, RELATIVE TO IMPROVING SIDEWALKS.

Be it ordained by the Mayor, Recorder and Aldermen of the City of Ann Arbor:

That Ordinance number fifteen entitled " An Ordinance rela-

"tive to improving Sidewalks," made and passed in Common Council on the twenty second day of March, in the year eighteen hundred and fifty three, be and the same is hereby amended by inserting between the words "the" and "owners" in the second line of the first section of said ordinance the word " resident."

Made and passed in Common Council at the City of Ann Arbor, the 17th day of October, A. D. 1859.

E. B. POND, President, *pro tem.*

N. E. WELCH, Recorder.

No. 39.

AN ORDINANCE AMENDATORY OF SECTIONS 7 AND 8 OF ORDINANCE NO. 4.

Be it ordained by the Mayor, Recorder and Aldermen of the City of Ann Arbor;

Sec. 1. That Section seven of said Ordinance No. 4, entitled "An Ordinance relative to the prevention of fires," passed in Common Council on the 17th day of June, A. D. 1851, be and the same is hereby amended by inserting after the word "fire-arms" in said section 7, the words "except cannon."

Sec. 2. That Section eight of said Ordinance No. 4 be and the same is hereby amended by striking out said section, and inserting in place thereof the following :

Sec. 8. Every person who shall fire a cannon within the limits of said City of Ann Arbor, and every person who shall aid or assist in the firing or causing to be fired any cannon within said limits, and every person accessory before the fact to the firing of any cannon within said limits, shall forfeit and pay a fine of one hundred dollars or be imprisoned in the common jail of the County of Washtenaw for the term of 30 days, or shall be punished by both fine and imprisonment ; and in case of prosecution under this section, half of the fine collected of any such person shall be paid to the informer who shall make complaint and institute such prosecution.

Made and passed in Common Council this 2d day of July, A. D. 1860.

ROBERT J. BARRY, Mayor.

D. S. TWITCHELL, Recorder.

No. 40.

AN ORDINANCE RELATIVE TO COLLECTOR.

Be it ordained by the Mayor, Recorder and Aldermen of the City of Ann Arbor:

That the qualified electors of the City of Ann Arbor, at the election to be held on the first Monday in April, and at each annual election thereafter, shall elect, by ballot, one Collector for the City of Ann Arbor,

Made and passed in Common Council this 11th day of March, A. D, 1861.

ROBERT J. BARRY, Mayor.

D. S. TWITCHELL, Recorder.